WJ
BOOKS

ISBN: 978-0-9576167-4-5

WANTED
A Leopold Blake Thriller

By Nick Stephenson

Nowhere to hide…

What should have been a relaxing vacation in Paris turns into another unwinnable situation for expert criminology consultant Leopold Blake. Caught in the cross hairs of a ruthless assassin and on the run from the police for a murder he didn't commit, Blake and his team must fight to clear his name before it's too late.

As enemies close in from all sides, Blake is about to learn who he can trust – and who is determined to destroy him – as The City of Light becomes a new hunting ground.

WJ
BOOKS

About the Author

Nick Stephenson was born and raised in Cambridgeshire, England. He writes mysteries, thrillers, and suspense novels, as well as the occasional witty postcard, all of which are designed to get your pulse pounding. His approach to writing is to hit hard, hit fast, and leave as few spelling errors as possible. Don't let his headshot fool you – he's actually full color (on most days).

His books are a mixture of mystery, action and humor, and are recommended for anyone who enjoys fast paced writing with plenty of twists and turns.

For up to date promotions and release dates of upcoming books, sign up for the latest news here:

Author Page: www.nickstephensonbooks.com

For William.

WANTED

A Leopold Blake Thriller

PROLOGUE: TWO WEEKS AGO

The hazmat suit was stifling and Luca Ginelli could barely catch his breath as he studied the monitors. Thanks to the research laboratory's state-of-the-art microsphere nanoscope, the young lab technician could easily study particles as small as one nanometer in diameter – the equivalent of one billionth of a meter – with unprecedented clarity.

The current specimen, a cluster of lung cells harvested from a pig, was no exception. He could easily make out the cell membranes, the nuclei, and even the tiny mitochondria that came together to form one of the most basic building blocks of animal life. But there was no time to stop and enjoy the view.

With a steady hand, Ginelli introduced a sample of nanoparticles to the viewing plate and increased the magnification. Despite being many times smaller than the pig cells, the nanoparticles moved much faster – making their way toward the membranes that protected the larger bodies with surprising speed. Within a few seconds they had reached their targets and set to work. Ginelli stared at the monitors in disbelief.

This isn't supposed to happen.

After years of research, nearly half a decade of refining, he was still no closer to a breakthrough. Instead of developing a revolutionary technique for locating and destroying cell mutations, all Ginelli had to show for his efforts was something even worse than the cancers he was trying to cure. If that weren't enough, senior management was now demanding daily progress reports and the pressure was starting to build. His workload had increased to the point where sleeping at the labs and starting work at dawn had become the only way to keep up. But what could be done about it?

Company morale was at an all-time low and Ginelli had heard whispers of strike action among the other employees. He knew nothing would come of it, everyone was too afraid of what might happen, but it was always a popular topic of conversation. That, and the myriad of conspiracy theories surrounding their work – theories that seemed to get less farfetched as time passed.

What if the theories aren't just theories? Ginelli's head swam with a variety of scenarios, each leading him back to the same question: *What exactly are we trying to create here?*

He took one last look at the monitor and shuddered. Shutting off the equipment, the young technician made his way through to the decontamination chamber and changed back into his lab clothes. As he pulled on his white lab coat, he took out his cell phone and took a long hard look at the screen. It would be easy enough to get in touch with someone, maybe talk to them about some of the concerns he and the others had. He didn't have to give them his name. Management would never find out.

With a final glance around him, Ginelli turned out the lights and made his way toward his sleeping quarters, checking his watch and wondering whether it was too late to make a quick phone call.

ONE: TODAY

Dieter Reiniger pictured the scene in his head and allowed himself a smile. Screaming through the air at nearly three thousand feet per second, the custom-made .338 bullet would punch through his target's skull as though it were made of paper, ensuring an instant kill with minimum fuss. The mark would be dead before he even heard the gunshot.

Perched high above Paris' Notre Dame square, the assassin had found it easy to slip away from his tour group unnoticed and had made his way to the very top of the ancient cathedral's Gothic parapets, giving him the perfect vantage point to carry out his mission.

Thirty stories below, hundreds of people milled around the expansive plaza, completely unaware of the danger lurking so high above them. A good portion of the unsuspecting souls were dressed in business attire, probably waiting for a lunch table at any one of the overpriced restaurants nearby, while the rest were clearly tourists hoping to soak up some of the city's famous landmarks. Dozens of Asian, American, and European holidaymakers huddled around the entrance to the famous cathedral waiting for their chance to see the impressive interior, while others took advantage of the public restrooms or chased their hyperactive children through the dense lunchtime hustle.

The summer season had truly begun in earnest, and the baking sun glistened enthusiastically over the surface of the River Seine, catching on the waves and reflecting off the brilliant white tour boats that cruised up and down the waterways. Reiniger took a deep breath through his nostrils and savored the clean air, glad for the chance to get away from the noise and pollution of street level.

The assassin knelt, unclasping the heavy Samsonite luggage he had carried up to the roof with him, and dug deep underneath a layer of carefully folded clothes to the hidden compartment installed at the bottom. Inside, the components of a modified AX338 sniper rifle were strapped tight to the case's toughened frame, and he caught the faint smell of gun oil as he leaned in close to remove the parts. He checked each component carefully and assembled the high-powered weapon in less than thirty seconds, laying the rifle by his feet once he had finished. He turned his attention to the ammunition.

Reiniger fished out six low-drag rounds from a small holster disguised as a glasses case and inspected them for any defects. Satisfied, he slipped them into his shirt pocket and closed up the bulky suitcase, making his way over to the edge of the roof and the two hundred foot drop below. At this elevation, the German could see across most of Paris and he gave himself a moment to soak up the glorious view. Facing west, he could make out the looming gray silhouette of the Eiffel Tower in the distance, one of only a handful of structures in the center of the capital that were taller than the cathedral itself. A little further on, just about visible on the outskirts of the city, the skyscrapers of the La Defense financial district glittered in the sunshine.

Taking up a position flat on his belly next to a particularly grotesque gargoyle, Reiniger flipped open the lens cap on the rifle's long range scope and peered through the glass. A little over a thousand feet away, he could clearly make out the steps leading up from the subterranean Notre Dame metro station as though he were standing just a few paces from it and he adjusted the lens to ensure the focus was perfect. The constant pour of commuters streaming out of the tunnels would make his target difficult to hit, but the assassin was prepared for that. All he had to do was breathe, focus, and take his time – and the rifle would do the rest.

Thankfully, the ambient conditions were perfect. The hot, humid air was the optimum density for working with a rifle and wind speed was minimal, meaning there was very little chance of a bullet veering off course. After the job was done, the suitcase would be left on the cathedral roof for the police to find, allowing the German a speedy getaway down the narrow staircase and onto the streets below with the rifle packed up in its carry case and slung over his shoulder.

Closing the lens cap to avoid giving away his position in the bright sun, Reiniger allowed himself to relax and thought back to his mission briefing. The client, some balding American, had been nervous, as most usually were, but he was very clear about one thing: it wasn't enough for the assassin to simply kill the targets. The client had tossed a set of photographs across the table and explained the objectives. It all sounded simple enough, Reiniger had said, before immediately doubling his price. The American had agreed. Perhaps a little too easily.

While this was no ordinary job, all the preparations had been made, payment had been received as usual, and the escape route was all mapped out. The only thing left to do was wait and keep watch. In just a few short hours, Dieter Reiniger would be well on the way to getting his hands on the last paycheck he would ever need.

TWO

Juliet Reno had waited in line at the Louvre for more than an hour. After standing outside in the baking lunchtime heat, the cool blast of the air conditioning inside the Renaissance Gallery was a welcome reprieve. As a third year Art History major, Juliet knew her Michelangelos from her Raphaels, but something about the sprawling museum always brought her back for more. As the crowds began to wane during the lunchtime rush, the young student found herself enjoying the rare luxury of an undisturbed stroll down the impressive hallways.

Without the usual hordes of tourists spoiling her view, Juliet allowed herself more time than usual to walk through the giant corridors, pausing several times along the way to soak up the finer details of some of the world's most famous masterpieces. As she reached a particularly impressive Mantegna, a young man with scruffy hair sidled up next to her, clearly as engrossed in the painting as she was. The stranger glanced over at her and smiled.

"Do you know this oil painting?" he asked in an American accent.

"Yes, of course," she replied, her English accented but otherwise flawless. "Da Vinci's 'The Virgin and Child with Saint Anne'."

"Anyone can read the plaque," the stranger said. "What's more interesting to me is whether you have any opinions of your own. What does this painting say to you?"

Juliet took a step back. "What makes you think I want to answer your questions?"

"You're an art student, right?"

"Yes? How did you know?"

"I watched you examine nearly every painting in this hall before you settled on this one. Nobody your age takes so long wandering the hallways leading up to the Mona Lisa. Most just charge straight on through. So, tell me about this painting. Tell me what it means to you."

Juliet folded her arms. "Okay, so you have a good eye. We know that Da Vinci painted this in the early sixteenth century, and it depicts the infant Christ grappling with a sacrificial lamb while his mother tries to restrain him."

"Yes, yes – these are the figures in the painting, but what does it *mean* to you?"

"The Virgin Mary appears to be sitting on Saint Anne's lap," Juliet continued, "which I suppose suggests some kind of strong bond between the two women. Perhaps a maternal relationship, much like the relationship between Mary and Jesus. To me, this is a scene of love and family – but with the foreshadowing of Christ's eventual death symbolized by the lamb. It is at once comforting and very disturbing."

"Good, very good. You're aware of the Freudian interpretation?"

"Of course. Freud theorized that the Virgin's cloak painted here," she traced the outline with her finger, just a few inches from the frame, "was designed to represent the shape of a bird of prey that Leonardo Da Vinci had dreamed of. A dream, Freud argued, that suggested latent homosexual tendencies in the young painter. Of course, for Freud, everything is about the penis, isn't it?"

He grinned. "Sometimes he has a point. And like many Da Vinci paintings, you'll notice the horizons are at different levels on each side of the main figure's head."

"Yes, like the Mona Lisa, it's the first thing most people notice. The technique is used to draw the eye to certain parts of the painting. In this case it pulls us in to focus on the face of Mary, so that we almost don't notice Saint Anne holding her up. Here, Da Vinci portrays a very strong figure, but one that keeps very much to the background. He had tremendous respect for her, I think."

"And you are aware of the more recent controversies?"

Juliet shook her head, wondering where this conversation was going. *Is he going to ask me out or something?* she thought, wondering what she would say if he did.

"In 2011 the painting was removed from the display to be cleaned and restored," he continued. "However, the work carried out on the oil paints caused the work to become brighter and more vibrant than before. Many argued this was not the artist's original intention.

There was quite an uproar. I'm surprised you didn't read about it."

"It was a little before my time," she replied, pushing back a strand of hair. "But why are you so interested?"

"It's my job to pay attention."

"And what job is that?"

"I get paid to notice things. I get paid even more to keep them to myself. Sometimes, I'm faced with a situation where I'm compelled to tell the secrets that I know. Today is one of those situations."

"Very mysterious," Juliet said. "And just what secrets do you have today?"

"I suppose I can best illustrate with this," he replied, pointing to the Da Vinci. "You can see where the artist has used such a muted palette?" he waited for her to nod. "Good, then you'll also see where the dust and other atmospheric particulates have accumulated over the years the whites and grays have become slightly inconsistent across the scene. They are brighter in some places than in others. A product of natural aging."

"Yes, very common."

"So, if the painting was cleaned and restored in 2011, why does this painting look like it hasn't been touched in hundreds of years?"

Juliet opened her mouth to reply, but couldn't find the right words. For the first time she could remember, the young student found herself speechless.

"The secret, you see," the scruffy man stepped forward until he was just a few inches from the elaborate golden frame, "is that any good restorer will leave in certain details of the painting that the artist intended to preserve. The color palette, for example. With this painting, however," he reached out gently and touched the wood of the frame, "the restoration team screwed up and brightened everything too much. Meaning whatever's hanging here today…"

Too late to stop him, Juliet lunged forward as the stranger wrenched the priceless masterpiece off the wall, setting off the security systems and filling the cavernous hall with a piercing klaxon alarm. The other visitors still meandering through the corridors froze as a security guard burst through the doors at the far end of the hallway and sprinted toward the cause of the disturbance.

"Meaning whatever's hanging here today," the stranger continued as though nothing unusual had happened, "is a fake. A very good one, but definitely a fake – one that was based on how the painting looked *before* the restoration messed with all the colors. In short, this doesn't belong here." He hoisted the frame up over his head and began to walk away. "Thank you for the conversation, but I need to be going. The art director is going to have a few questions. I'm sure this gentleman will be kind enough to escort me," he nodded toward the security officer running in their direction.

"Who are you?" said Juliet, stepping away.

"Of course, where are my manners?" he held out his hand. "Leopold Blake. Nice to meet you."

Eyes wide, Juliet shook the young man's hand and watched dumbstruck as he carried the painting toward the exit.

THREE

The piercing noise woke Mary Jordan at seven A.M. with a jolt, interrupting a particularly violent dream. Fumbling in the dark, the NYPD police sergeant felt across her nightstand for the alarm clock and succeeded in knocking over her lamp. Still half asleep, she located the offending device and slammed her palm down on the snooze button.

For the fourth morning in a row Mary had fallen asleep fully dressed and, after two full weeks of working nights, the seasoned cop had reached her limit. New York's finest had trained her to deal with violent criminals, perverts, and street gangs, but nothing had prepared her for fourteen days with no sleep. Resisting the urge to groan, Mary swung her feet out over the side of the bed and stumbled into the bathroom, pulling off her crumpled clothes and tossing them onto the floor. She turned on the shower and waited for the pipes to stop rattling before stepping into the cubicle, letting the hot water do its work.

Thoroughly scrubbed, she wrapped a towel around herself and stepped out of the shower to inspect herself in the mirror. Wiping the condensation away with her palm, she forced her eyes open. The results were not good. Swearing under her breath, she rummaged through her bathroom cupboards and eventually located her makeup bag behind a stack of Xanax bottles. She fished out the bag of lotions and powders and dumped the whole thing on the edge of the sink.

After a cursory layer of foundation had covered up the worst of the damage, Mary headed back to the bedroom. She threw on something warm and comfortable – a nice change from her usual duty uniform – and fished out the airline tickets and passport from her underwear drawer. In less than two hours her flight would be boarding, which didn't leave much time for packing.

Mary's cell phone let out a muffled chirp from the corner of the room. Digging out the handset from underneath a pile of old case reports, she saw the caller ID flash up and sighed.

"Mom, this isn't a good time," she said, pulling her suitcase out of her closet with one hand and opening it on the bed.

"I know sweetheart, it's just always so difficult to catch you at a good one. Are you in the middle of something?" Her mother's voice was a little more strained than usual.

"What's wrong, mom? You never call me unless it's bad news."

"That's not true. I called you last month. You know, before you were called away on that case. What was that all about again?"

"Never mind. It doesn't matter. It's good to hear from you."

"It's nice to hear your voice too. But you know we need to have that talk."

"I can't right now," said Mary, throwing clothes into the empty case. "I've got a flight to catch."

"Oh, that sounds exciting. For work?"

"No, vacation. I've got five days saved up that I need to use."

"Vacation? It's about time they gave you some time off. Not that you can afford to go anywhere nice on your salary. You know, Annie's son Marcus still has connections at his firm. Maybe –"

Mary cut her off. "Forget it, mom. I don't work homicide for the money."

"I should hope not."

"Besides, I deserve a vacation. I've got a little cash saved up, there's no reason I shouldn't use it."

"Going anywhere nice?"

"Paris," said Mary. "The one in France. I'll be eating baguettes and croissants for a whole week, and I won't have to worry about anyone trying to shoot at me. I'm looking forward to it."

"France, huh? Very romantic. And who are you going with? Not by yourself, I assume?"

"I'm flying out alone. I'll be meeting up with a… um, friend, when I arrive. An old friend."

"Mary, honey, not this guy you're always talking about? You know he's nothing but trouble."

"I'll be fine, mom," Mary rolled her eyes. "I'm a big girl. I can look after myself. Listen, I'm already running late and I need to find a cab."

"All right sweetie, I'll let you get on with packing. But we still need to have that talk. It's very important."

"I know, mom. I promise we'll talk soon, okay?"

"Sure, honey. Fly safe and I'll call you in a couple of days."

Mary heard a soft click as her mother hung up the phone, leaving her alone to finish a hurried search for clean clothes and suitable footwear.

After ten frenetic minutes, Mary emerged from her apartment building onto the New York streets and flagged down a cab. At seven thirty A.M. the sun was rising and Mary could already feel the hints of a scorching day ahead as she climbed into the taxi and buckled her seatbelt. The driver nodded as she gave him her destination and the cab made its way along Broadway, which was already busy enough with commuters to make progress painfully slow.

Holding up the boarding pass she'd printed the night before, she forced herself to relax. Ignoring the mounting crescendo of city noise outside, she imagined herself sat in a small Parisian café enjoying the sunshine with a plate of French pastries and a chilled glass of white wine. She could almost taste the hot, flaky *pain au chocolat*. With a satisfied smile, Mary folded the boarding pass and slipped it into her pocket. A grumble from her stomach reminded her to find some breakfast once she had checked in and wondered whether Newark airport served *mille-feuille*. She quickly dismissed the thought and resigned herself to the possibility of a stale bagel instead.

FOUR

Leopold Blake was handcuffed to a steel chair when Jean Dubois – the Louvre's senior art director – burst into the room. Slamming the door behind him, the old man stomped across the office toward the consultant. The ceiling light swayed in protest, casting strange shadows across the floor.

"*Merde!* What the hell do you think you are doing?" Dubois said.

"Calm down," said Leopold. "You hired me to perform a full security sweep of this place. I did my job, nothing more, *Monsieur* Dubois." He felt his right arm go numb where the handcuffs were too tight.

"The Musée du Louvre commissioned you to perform a full audit of this gallery's anti-theft systems," said Dubois. "We did *not* pay you to go around and steal paintings from our walls."

"The museum is owned by the French government, right?"

"*Oui*, what of it?"

"And why do you think the French government would hire an American to consult on their security arrangements?"

"Well, I don't know why they would. Maybe they –"

"They contacted me," Leopold interrupted, "because I'm the best at what I do. I've worked as a criminology expert and consultant for more than a dozen national and international agencies, which is where I believe your bosses found my contact details."

"I still don't understand why –"

"Why this is relevant? Because your boss was recommended my services directly by the FBI Director, that's why. I agreed to take the job because it makes a nice change from the usual homicide cases and it means I can spend a week in Paris not getting shot at."

"Then why try to steal a painting? What are you trying to prove?"

Leopold sighed. "I could have waited. I could have filed the report, as you requested. But I'm not a big fan of paperwork, and I wanted to get the message across quickly. And here we are."

"And where are we?"

"We're in your security team's holding office and I'm telling you that the Louvre is missing one Da Vinci painting."

"The one you tried to steal?"

"We've been through this," he rubbed his eyes with his free hand. "The painting I pulled down is a fake. A masterful copy, no doubt, but a fake nonetheless. I opted for the more direct approach of getting your attention, rather than scheduling an appointment – by which time your art thief could have had a chance to escape. Are you keeping up?"

Dubois scowled. "How do you know it's a fake?"

"You have eyes, don't you? Go talk to the curator. She was a little more receptive to my assistance."

The old man swallowed. "So let's say I agree with you. What do we do next?"

"*We* do nothing, *Monsieur*. I, on the other hand, will find out who on your staff is behind the theft and work with you to recover the original. After that, you can have my thoughts on the rest of your security systems as originally promised."

"You think this was one of my staff?"

"No doubt about it. There's no other explanation for how the painting could have been switched without someone noticing. This must be an inside job."

"We only commissioned you to examine the systems. You really think you can help?"

"Of course – it's what I do. And it's why people like the FBI Director feel comfortable in recommending me to other agencies. I don't do this for the money, you know."

"It's not like you need it, Mr. Blake," Dubois straightened his tie. "I've read all about you in the papers. I must say, I was expecting someone, erm, how do you say?"

"Different."

"*Oui, oui,*" the director eyed Leopold quizzically, "*different* is the word, for sure. So what can I do to help?"

"You can start by getting me out of these cuffs. Once you've done that, call an all-employee meeting and get everyone whose job involves handling any of the artwork down to a meeting room as soon as you can. I have a feeling whoever is responsible for this will panic and slip up if we apply just the right pressure. We just need to know where to look."

"*Bien sûr*, no problem. I'll be back with the keys in a moment."

Director Dubois stalked out of the tiny office and Leopold heard his footsteps echo down the hallway and out of earshot.

FIVE

The *Thanatos* swept noiselessly through the chilly Atlantic waters, holding a steady speed of twenty-eight knots. The 312 foot customized yacht had been retrofitted with state-of-the-art propulsion systems and anti-radar graphite panels that covered its outer hull, meaning at two hundred miles from shore the chances of being tracked and followed were almost zero. With over forty million dollars' worth of high-tech surveillance and covert interception equipment, The *Thanatos* was easily the most networked private vessel on the planet.

Senior Operative James Cullen sat in the middle of the bustling command center, surrounded by smart glass walls, a type of privacy material that uses electro-chromatic technology to switch between transparent and translucent states by applying current. Squinting at the reams of text flowing across his bank of computer monitors, the senior operative noticed something strange and paused the data feed, leaning in closer to get a better look. There, pulsing gently on the high-resolution screen, was a name. A name that Cullen had seen crop up at least six times in the last twenty-four hours.

Rubbing his eyes, he checked the data logs for the last week and a summary of keyword activity flashed up on the screen. Sure enough, the name had been flagged up by the interceptor systems over three dozen times in the last seven days, which was almost unheard of.

Why the hell wasn't I informed? Cullen thought, reaching for the telephone. He paused as he lifted the receiver, his gut once again telling him something wasn't quite right. *The Director is hiding something.*

For nearly ten years James Cullen had worked for The Organization, quickly promoted into a senior position following his tenure at one of the permanent bases in South Africa. Recruited straight out of MIT, a six-figure starting salary had been all the incentive Cullen had needed to keep his questions regarding the finer details of his new employer to himself. The tradeoff had been a happy one. In return for unquestioning loyalty and a military approach to obeying orders, the young college graduate had been given wealth, opportunity, and a life spent traveling the globe. Still, The Director had never kept anything from him before.

I need some outside perspective.

Cullen adjusted the Smart Glass into transparency mode and blinked hard as the crowded command center sprang into view. A dozen operatives of varying seniority scurried about the open-plan room, while others remained seated at their desks punching data into their computers and speaking into headset microphones. At the far end of the office, Cullen could make out the bright blonde hair of Rose Carter, a junior officer with whom he had struck up a friendship. The two of them had hit it off immediately and, of all the souls on board, he knew he could always trust her for an honest opinion. Cullen picked up the phone once again and punched in Rose's extension.

"James, what can I do for you?" a bright, friendly voice answered. "I wasn't sure I'd be hearing from you after the beating you took last night."

Cullen laughed. "We can't all have your luck with the nine ball, can we?"

"Okay, so maybe pool's not your game," she said. "What's up? You must have been down here a while."

"You had breakfast yet?"

"No. I was planning on hitting the canteen at eight thirty."

"It's nearly nine now, Rose. Lost in your work again?"

Rose chuckled. "You'll have to remember that next time you're writing your performance reviews. I'm guessing you want to grab a bite?"

"I hear they've got leftover bagels," said Cullen, feeling his stomach gurgle. "If we're quick, we might get a couple before the chefs finish them off. Plus, I've got something I want to run by you."

"Sure, sounds good. Anything serious?"

"No, I just need someone to bounce a couple ideas off, that's all."

"Another one of your hunches?" asked Rose. "You know those only ever get you into trouble."

"Don't I know it. Anyway, lock up your workstation and get over here. We've not got long before they close up the kitchens and I'm starving."

"Yes, boss."

Cullen watched the young operative tidy her desk and make her way over to his office. She walked with a confidence that matched her striking looks, and Cullen noticed at least a couple of stray glances from the men in the room as she strode past.

"Ready, boss?" she poked her head through the door.

"You bet. Let me lock up my computer."

A few swift keystrokes later, and Cullen was on his feet and leading the way toward the canteen. As the pair made their way through the brightly lit corridors, Cullen tried to calm the sudden uneasiness in his stomach and prayed his innate knack for sensing trouble wasn't about to make him throw up. Rose opened the door to the canteen and waved Cullen through, who was still lost in his own thoughts.

"You doing all right, boss?" she asked, grabbing a tray from the shelf and making her way to the serving station. "Something on your mind?"

"Yes, you could say that," Cullen replied, following suit. "You're sworn to secrecy though, the usual drill."

"Of course," Carter replied, helping herself to a glass of orange juice. "I've trusted you enough times in the past. My lips are sealed."

Cullen grabbed a bagel and a packet of cream cheese before making his way to an empty table. Rose followed, grabbing two cups of coffee from the nearby dispenser.

"Black, no sugar," she smiled, sliding the hot drink across the table to him.

"Thanks. I don't get how you can drink it with all that nasty powdered milk."

"Adds flavor," she replied, taking a big sip. "So, what's up, Doc?"

Cullen took a gulp of his coffee and glanced around the canteen, glad the place was deserted. "I've been tracking the current initiatives and something's not feeling quite right."

"What do you mean?"

"Usually, my involvement in any one project is minimal. I mean, sure, I'm aware of what's going on in the broadest sense, but I only really need to know the headline points."

"Yeah, I get that. Too much going on to get bogged down in the detail. That's why people like me are here, right?"

"Yeah, exactly. But what gets me is that I make a point of being aware of any major development that could affect us. And, until this morning, I had no reason to think that I was missing out."

"And now you do?" asked Rose, draining the last of her coffee and taking a large bite out of her bagel.

"That's what my gut is telling me."

"Any particular reason?"

Cullen sighed. "I didn't want to get you involved in anything that might get us both into trouble."

"Relax," she said, taking another chomp of her breakfast. "It's just you and me in here. Speak away."

After a long pause, he made up his mind and nodded. "Okay, but this is just a hunch, remember. There might not be anything to it."

"Spit it out, already!"

"Let me put it this way…" Cullen tapped his fingers on the table. "During the last US election, how often would you guess our systems would pick up a hit with the President's name listed as a keyword?"

"I'm not sure. Our systems aggregate world news across the whole of the web, and only spit out unique content that's relevant to our ongoing initiatives. So, out of millions of internet results, our systems might only filter through a few dozen."

"Right. The answer to my question, by the way, is forty. In the week leading up to the last election, our systems registered only forty relevant hits – and that's out of more than a billion news stories around the world."

"Okay, I get where you're going with this. Our systems have picked up on something, or *someone*, that you're not already aware of?"

"Tell me," he said, lowering his voice to a whisper. "Does the name Leopold Blake mean anything to you?"

SIX

The air conditioning was broken and the meeting room had quickly warmed up with the mass of bodies assembled inside. Leopold stood at the far end of the room, watching the Louvre employees find a seat on the plastic chairs, while Dubois fiddled with a feeble-looking floor fan. After several attempts, Dubois managed to get the blades spinning, and aimed the airflow in the direction of the gathering crowd. As the mumblings and whispers began to fade, the old man leaned in close and caught Leopold's attention.

"I'm afraid I will have to leave you for a while," he said. "I have an... appointment across town, and I am already late. You will forgive me, *non?*"

Leopold nodded. "In fact, I'd prefer it. Without you in the room, people will relax a little."

"Then please excuse me." The director patted Leopold on the shoulder and made his way to the exit. "If you need me, try my cell phone."

"I will, thank you."

As the old man shuffled away, Leopold focused his attention on the employees gathered in front of him. He cleared his throat. "Thank you for coming," he said, projecting his voice to the back of the room. "I'm sure you're all wondering why you're here. Director Dubois has kindly arranged this impromptu meeting on my behalf, but he won't be joining us for the rest of the session." He scanned the faces in front of him for any signs of nervousness. "No doubt you heard the security systems going off earlier this morning. I'm here to talk to you a little bit about why that happened. My name is Leopold Blake, and I'm here as a security consultant for the Musée du Louvre. Any questions?"

Nobody responded.

"Excellent," said Leopold. "Then I'll get right down to it. The alarms were set off deliberately to test the systems, which all appear to be fully operational. What does concern me, however, is there is little or no record keeping where members of staff or outsiders come into contact with pieces of art or other valuable assets. In the private security business, this often represents the biggest vulnerability of any system – the *défaut de la cuirasse,* so to speak. Part of my work here will be designing a system that tracks and documents who comes into contact with Louvre property and what justifications they have for doing so."

A timid hand rose slowly at the back of the room.

"Yes?"

The hand's owner, a small, mousy woman with thick spectacles, stood up. "There are hundreds of employees who might have access to any area of the collections," she said. "Why ask only us to the meeting?"

"Good question," said Leopold. "Director Dubois informs me that your division is most likely to personally interact with the artwork, so naturally I wanted to get your feedback first. I understand the restoration department, the acquisitions team, and the archive group are all here?"

A few members of the audience nodded.

"Would the senior managers from each department please raise their hands?" asked Leopold.

Four hands shot up in the air.

"Excellent. Tell me, when was the last time anything was stolen from the museum's collections?"

One of the managers got to his feet, a balding man with a crumpled suit and a gray goatee.

"Nothing has been stolen from the Louvre for over a century," he announced, his accent German. "Not since the Mona Lisa debacle forced us to lock her up behind bulletproof glass. This is a secure facility, Mr. Blake. You should not come here and accuse us of being incompetent."

Taking a step forward, Leopold met the man's stare and raised his palms. "Believe me, accusing you of anything is the last thing I would want to do. I only want to use your expertise to help improve security, nothing more. I'm sure all you fine people only want to help make your nation's prized collections just a little bit safer."

The manager sat back down. "What do you want us to do?"

"This is the fun part," Leopold replied, smiling. "I want you to tell me how you would steal something from this museum, and exactly how you would expect to get away with it."

After a few moments of uncomfortable silence, several hands flew into the air at once and Leopold listened to his audience's suggestions. Most of the ideas were too outlandish to reveal any useful leads, including one proposal that a would-be thief might simply swap out the real painting for a print from the gift shop while nobody was looking.

After twenty minutes, Leopold gave up. "Okay, okay, I think I've heard enough for now. There were some great ideas today, which I'll be sure to include in my upcoming report."

"Will we get to read it?" asked the mousy woman, getting up from her seat again. "Or maybe we could act it out, *non?* We could form a team, and try to steal something ourselves?" She was practically bouncing up and down with excitement.

"That won't be necessary," said Leopold. "I have everything I need for the time being. *Merci, tout le monde,* for all your help. You can get back to work now." He gestured toward the door.

With a groan of disappointment, the employees got to their feet and shuffled out the main doors back to their offices. Once alone, Leopold took a deep breath, closed his eyes, and rubbed his temples.

As a plan began to form in the back of his mind, the consultant felt a heavy weight on his shoulder. Turning, he looked up into the eyes of an impossibly tall man, dressed in a well-tailored suit almost as dark as his coal-black skin. Despite the excellent cut of the jacket, Leopold could make out the outline of a handgun holstered to the man's ribs.

"Dammit, Jerome. I told you not to sneak up on me when I'm thinking," said Leopold, trying to recover his train of thought. You're paid to be my bodyguard. You don't get a fat paycheck every month in return for giving me a heart attack."

Jerome smiled. "It's all part of my training program. Find out anything useful?"

"Maybe. While this particular group might not be master criminals in the making, they did offer some insight into how the museum handles its more valuable pieces."

"Such as?"

"The most important works, like the Mona Lisa, for example, are visually inspected at the beginning and end of each day for damage. The painting in question, 'The Virgin and Child with Saint Anne', is inspected once every week."

"One of the inspection teams is responsible?"

"No, that would be too obvious. Although I'm sure the French police will want to question them, I'm certain they weren't the ones to make the switch. The real importance of the inspection schedules is that the thief must have known the counterfeit would have been discovered at the next check. After all, the difference in the color palette is quite obvious to anyone familiar with the story behind the botched restoration, which the inspection teams are sure to be."

"Meaning that whoever stole the original knew they'd get found out eventually?"

"Exactly. And, as I said to the director, this has to be an inside job," said Leopold, starting to move toward the exit. "And anyone working for the museum will want this whole affair to stay under the radar for as long as possible, which can only mean one thing."

"Always one for the dramatic, aren't you?" said Jerome, following his employer through the doors and into the corridor. "And what does it mean?"

"That the thief was planning to switch out the counterfeit painting with a more up to date knock off. One that the inspection team wouldn't notice is a fake."

"Let me guess; you've got a plan to track this person down?"

"It's quite simple. At least, it is now I've had chance to think. All we need to do is figure out who would routinely come into contact this particular piece while unsupervised and we've got enough evidence to start asking questions."

"Are you going straight to the police with this?"

"My contract is with the Musée du Louvre," said Leopold. "They can decide what to do with the information. I need to speak to the human resources department first, and then I'll give the director a call with my recommendations. Hopefully he'll be finished with his lunch date soon."

The bodyguard stepped up the pace a little and the pair hit the main lobby, illuminated from above by the sunshine streaming through the enormous glass pyramid that formed part of the museum's roof. After a muted conversation with one of the reception desk employees, the two men set off in the direction of the personnel offices, weaving their way though the tourists toward the HR department at the far end of the east wing.

"Looks like I've got some signal," announced Leopold, inspecting his cell phone as they crossed the cavernous atrium. "But the director's not picking up. We're on our own for now."

Jerome smiled as they passed through the reception area and into another long corridor. "Just the way you like it," he said, closing the door behind him.

SEVEN

Jean Dubois had forged a respectable career in the Paris art community over his forty two years in the business, and he was damned if he was going to let today's slipup tarnish his legacy. Something about the American consultant's sudden appearance just didn't sit right with him – after all, the museum hadn't run into issues for decades and Dubois couldn't fathom why the Louvre chairman would think some foreign stranger would know any better. The whole thing stank to high heaven, but, fortunately, the Musée du Louvre's ill-conceived bumblings wouldn't be his problem for much longer.

Having failed to flag down a taxi during the lunch time rush, Dubois resigned himself to taking the metro. Now, crammed into one of the city's many underground trains, the old director kept his eyes down and tried not to breathe in the stale, sweaty air as the carriage rumbled through the tunnels beneath the Le quai de l'Hôtel-de-Ville.

Glancing at his watch, he tried to keep himself from panicking. *This is not the time to be late*, he thought to himself as the train rounded a corner and forced him up against the window. *Not today. Not with everything that's going on.*

The news had come through only weeks earlier. The board of directors had voted in favor of Dubois' retirement at the end of the year, a move that forced him to reconsider his plans. The state pension from the French government was hardly enough to keep the old man in the lifestyle he had grown accustomed to, so drastic action would be needed to pad out his portfolio. And if that weren't enough, the American's recent discovery would cause an uproar once the news hit the national media. Dubois wasn't so naïve to think he'd escape the lion's share of the blame, meaning there was a strong chance he would find himself forced to resign, cutting his retirement funds even further.

They always need a scapegoat, he mused, bitterly.

Still, after his lunch meeting, things would start to look a little better. The director gripped the handrail a little tighter as the train rattled through a particularly dark tunnel before squealing to a halt at the Saint Michel – Notre Dame station. He shuffled his way through the packed carriage toward the doors, which slid open with a reluctant groan. Stepping out onto the busy platform, he dodged his way through the station with a renewed sense of urgency.

As he reached the concrete steps that led up to the main road, Dubois took a moment to compose himself before following the crowd up the stairs. Out on the streets, the director could make out the twin towers of Notre Dame Cathedral just a few hundred feet away, reaching up beyond a line of tall trees. Dubois stepped out onto the sidewalk and made a beeline for the plaza, where his meeting companions would no doubt be waiting for him.

Glancing down at his watch once again, the old man saw something from the corner of his eye. He squinted up at the cathedral, noticing a glimmer of light at the top of one of the towers, a tiny pinprick of light that was nonetheless bright enough to draw his attention.

What the hell?

As the high velocity round passed through his skull, Dubois experienced only a nanosecond of regret before his life vanished into blackness.

EIGHT

The recoil from the .338 Lapua Magnum round was mostly absorbed by the rifle's sturdy seventeen pound frame, but Reiniger could still feel the kick as the bullet tore out of the muzzle at three times the speed of sound. Within seconds of his first target hitting the floor, the panic had already started – meaning his next shots would be all the more difficult to make in the noise and commotion.

From his position at the top of the cathedral, Reiniger had a decent view of the plaza below and the metro station's subterranean stairwell a little further beyond. Taking a split second to catch his breath, the assassin peered through the scope for a second time and located his next target; a middle-aged woman wearing a frumpy summer top who was screaming at the top of her lungs next to the corpse of the first victim.

Allowing the air to leave his lungs in a slow, controlled exhale, Reiniger lined up his shot and felt himself moving in precise rhythm with the woman, feeling her movements curse through his body as though they were his own. He caressed the trigger and felt a jolt in his shoulder as the round left his weapon. Almost instantly, he saw the frumpy woman's head explode in a shower of crimson, her lifeless body twirling in mid-air before hitting the sidewalk.

Shutting out the noise of the crowd two hundred feet below him, Reiniger reloaded the bolt action AX338 in one quick, smooth motion, sliding a fresh round into the chamber. Through the scope, he saw his next target emerge from the station stairwell, bobbing up and down as he walked. The man wore a cheap suit and his face dropped to the floor as he stepped out into the sunshine. With a careful breath, Reiniger ended his life with a gentle squeeze of the trigger. The target buckled as the bullet tore through his chest and punched a hole in his abdomen the size of a basketball. Next, Reiniger felled a Japanese tourist who tried to run away. He hit the mark squarely in the neck, almost severing the man's head from his shoulders.

Ignoring a policeman who had sprinted onto the scene – it was always a bad idea to kill a cop – Reiniger spotted his final target emerge from the staircase, a skinny woman dressed in expensive clothes. He made the shot and she hit the ground hard, dead before she even realized what was happening. The assassin had brought his total to five kills in less than a minute.

Without pausing to observe the chaos, Reiniger wiped down the rifle with a rag and a squirt of ethanol before disassembling the weapon and zipping it up in the carry case. He repeated the cleanup job on his luggage, making sure to thoroughly scrub his DNA from every surface. Satisfied any trace of him had been removed, the German pulled a small metallic case from his pocket and opened the clasp to reveal a thin strip of transparent film. Holding the strip up to the sunlight, Reiniger could see the fingerprint branded onto the plastic. He knelt down next to the abandoned rifle and pressed the strip against one of the smoother pieces of stonework, hoping the porous surface would allow for a satisfactory impression.

With no time to inspect his work, Reiniger dashed across the roof of the tower and through the makeshift entryway into the cathedral's interior, making his way down the stairs to the belfry with the rifle case slung over his shoulder. He descended into the bell tower and caught the scent of old timber and iron as the cool air hit his nose. Thankful that the tour groups were restricted to the other tower, the assassin strode quickly and silently across the dusty floor toward the main stairs that led down to ground level, keeping his eyes locked ahead as he went.

His heart rate barely elevated, Reiniger reached the spectacular main hall in a little over thirty seconds, glad that his level of fitness kept him from looking out of breath. Ignoring the cathedral employees urging everyone to stay inside, the assassin strode toward the main doors and stepped out into the hot sun, keeping his eyes down. He wove in and out of the panicked crowd of tourists toward the Rue du Cloître, a quiet road that ran parallel to the cathedral.

The street was deserted, as expected, the majority of the pedestrians having run in the direction of the commotion – a human trait that Reiniger had never quite understood. The assassin kept moving, putting as much distance between him and the commotion as he could without breaking into a run.

"*Arrêtez!*" a voice shouted from somewhere behind him as he reached a shadier part of the road.

Reiniger slowed his pace and turned his head to see a policeman running in his direction, the same policeman he had seen in the rifle scope minutes earlier.

"Ou allez vous?" the cop demanded as he drew close: *where are you going?*

Reiniger noticed the policeman was unarmed, but he was wearing a radio. "You speak English?" the assassin asked, attempting to hide his German accent. He eyed the policeman's name tag, which read "Laurent."

The cop nodded. *"Oui.* Please stop walking, sir. I need to ask you to come with me please."

"I'm late for a lunch meeting, I'm afraid I need to be on my way. What's this all about?"

"Most people are trying to see what is going on, and you're worried about a lunch appointment? And what is that?" Officer Laurent pointed to the black carry case.

"Nothing important."

"I'll need to see your I.D. please."

"I don't have any on me, I'm sorry."

"Then you will need to come with me to the station. I can't have —"

Officer Laurent never had a chance to finish his sentence. With practiced speed, the assassin whipped out the KA-BAR clippoint knife hidden beneath his jacket and drove the steel blade into policeman's throat, twisting the handle as he withdrew. Reiniger wasted no time in shoving the cop into the bushes before the arterial blood could start spurting. Laurent's body fell silently through the foliage, hitting the soil with a muffled *thump* as Reiniger slipped the knife back to its sheath.

Glancing around to make sure nobody was watching, the assassin checked his clothes for any blood spatter and started walking once again, keen to get out of sight as quickly as possible. At the end of the block, Reiniger spotted his car – a black VW Passat with tinted windows and a fake license plate.

Climbing into the driver's seat, the assassin started the engine and rolled the car out onto the Rue du Cloître, keeping the speed under thirty. Reiniger crossed the nearby bridge onto Île Saint-Louis and soon found himself cruising along the main highway that led toward Charles de Gaulle Airport, a thirty minute drive away. As the dominating view of the cathedral recessed into the distance, Reiniger allowed himself a flicker of a smile.

Just one more loose end to tie up.

NINE

The scruffy Montmartre backstreets were overlooked by the white dome of the Basilica of the Sacré Cœur, which sat atop the highest point in the whole of Paris. Most of the summer crowds were milling around the grassy lawns at the base of the hill, while others sat on the steps, taking advantage of the sunshine and fresh air while they finished their packed lunches and watched their children run up and down the stairs.

Leopold and Jerome trekked deeper into the trendy neighborhood, grateful for the cool shade offered by the terraced apartment buildings. Most of the architecture was old, slightly worn, but nonetheless possessing a charm that was unique to the French capital.

"It should be just up here," said Jerome, inspecting the GPS display on his cell phone. "Less than a minute's walk."

The discussion with the personnel department at the Louvre had been quicker than Leopold had expected, and the information they needed had been handed over without much fuss. Apparently, namedropping director Dubois opened a lot of doors. Having an armed bodyguard along for the ride didn't hurt, either. The clerk had printed out a short list of names based on the consultant's criteria, and Leopold had picked the most likely match: an employee with the art restoration department who had called in sick for the last few days.

"We're looking for the number nineteen," said Leopold, wiping his brow with the back of his sleeve. "Apartment number three."

"Sophie Bardot," nodded Jerome. "We got a picture?"

"No, the clerk only printed out the name and address. If she doesn't answer, we'll camp out and wait for her." He pointed at a café a little further down the street, nestled on the corner with the familiar Parisian canopy and outdoor chairs.

"Definitely more comfortable than staking out a place in the car. Here we are."

They walked up to one of the terraced apartment blocks and Leopold hit the buzzer. After the third jab, a voice crackled into life through the intercom.

"*Oui, vous aider?*" the voice asked.

Leopold leaned in to the grille. "Mademoiselle Bardot?"

A short pause. "*Oui?*"

"*Parlez-vous anglais?*" he asked. *Do you speak English?*

"Yes. Who is this?"

"My name is Leopold Blake. My associate and I are here from the New York Art Review Magazine. We were hoping to catch you at work, but the museum said you would be at home. We found your address online." He waited for a response, hoping the lie would hold.

A short pause. "And what can I help you with?"

"We hoped to trouble you for a short interview. It would be a great opportunity for us to create a candid behind the scenes look at what goes on behind the walls of the Louvre. We want to show the world your talents, Mlle. Bardot. Will you spare us a few minutes?"

Another pause. "*Pardon,* I am not feeling too well. Please give me one moment."

"Of course."

After almost a minute of silence, "*D'accord.* You can come on up. Third floor."

With a loud buzz, the door lock disengaged and the consultant pushed through into the communal hallway, a dark, cool passage sparsely decorated with white paint and a tile floor. The old wooden stairs leading up to Sophie's apartment were toward the back of the room, and the steps creaked with over a century's worth of warping as they climbed.

On the third floor Sophie Bardot was waiting, a tall, slim, young-looking woman with jet black hair and green eyes. She was dressed in a pair of loose fitting jeans and a printed tee shirt, and wore a look of impatience on her otherwise attractive face.

"Mlle. Bardot?" offered Leopold. "May we come inside?"

Nodding, Sophie waved them both inside and shut the door. Her apartment was outfitted in typical Parisian style, most of the furniture looked as though it had been reclaimed from junk yards and garage sales. The living area was small, just about big enough for a couch and armchair, with a bookshelf containing a few scattered titles and a kitchenette separated from the main room by an archway. An open window facing out onto the city took up most of the back wall, framed by a set of thin curtains that billowed gently in the breeze.

Thanks to the elevation, the view over Paris was spectacular.

"Please, take a seat," said Sophie. "Let me fetch you something to drink."

"That would be perfect."

Their hostess smiled, all traces of irritation gone. She fetched a large jug of pale lemonade from the fridge and nestled it on the tiny coffee table along with three glasses. She poured out three generous measures before helping herself, settling back into the armchair. Leopold took a sip. The flavors were magnificent, with just enough sugar to take the edge off without being too sweet.

"Thank you, it's delicious," he said, raising his glass. "Do you mind if we begin the interview?"

"Of course. Ask your questions."

"Okay, first of all, tell me about your role at the museum. What is it that an art restorer does, exactly?"

Sophie sat up in her chair, taking a long sip of lemonade. "Most of the paintings in the Renaissance galleries are exposed to the atmosphere. It is only for a very select few pieces, such as the Mona Lisa, that we go to the expense of sealing them in an airtight UV-filtered case. Because of this, most of the artwork will begin to deteriorate over time as the moisture and sunlight gets into the paint. My job at the gallery is to clean and restore the paintings, as well as to preserve and protect them for the future."

"And which paintings are sent to you?"

"Each of the oil paintings in the renaissance galleries is cleaned and restored on a rotating schedule, depending on the requirements of the piece in question. It can often take weeks to carry out the work required, especially if the painting is damaged, so I find myself busy most of the time. The smaller paintings can be restored by just one person, usually me, but the larger more valuable ones often require a team of experts."

"And what work needs doing when you get these paintings through?"

"The usual problems are surface dirt, discoloration and cracked paint. Though, occasionally, the damage can be more severe on the older and more fragile works. It's nothing I can't handle, though."

"And so modest, too," said Leopold, smiling.

"*Monsieur* Blake," she replied, leaning forward in her chair, "I have spent over a decade learning the styles of the Old Masters. I doubt there is anyone who has an eye for detail quite like mine."

Leopold sipped his lemonade and set the glass down on the coffee table. "Are you aware of the recent theft from the museum, Mlle. Bardot?"

"There hasn't been a theft from the museum in decades. Where are you getting your information?"

"I have my sources. 'The Virgin and Child with St Anne' is missing. In its place, a reproduction." Leopold pulled out his cell phone and held up a picture of the painting. "The colors are all wrong. Since the last restoration, the palette is much brighter. Do you know who could have pulled something like this off?"

"*C'est impossible!* This is a joke, *non?*"

"I'm afraid not, Mlle. Bardot. Please, can you offer any insight?"

She took the cell phone from Leopold and held it up to her face. "This is not the true work of Da Vinci," she deferred, zooming in on the image. "Even on a digital camera like this, I can tell."

"Who could have taken the original?"

"Only somebody with enough influence over the board to have the displays moved," she replied. "The painting would have to be moved into the back rooms. Otherwise, the security cameras would have picked something up."

"When was the last time you saw the painting yourself?"

"Just a few weeks ago during a routine inspection. I signed everything off as satisfactory. Since then, I guess the frame was returned to its display in the gallery."

"Is there any possibility it was intercepted on the way?"

"Again, only someone senior could arrange for –" she stopped mid sentence.

"What is it?" pressed Leopold. "Any information you have could be important."

Sophie shook her head. "*Non*, it is just a coincidence."

"If you don't tell us, you'll only make it harder for the police. You don't want anything to happen to the painting, do you?"

She bit her lip thoughtfully. "There have been whispers. Especially with the news that Jean, I mean, *Monsieur* Dubois, was pushed into early retirement. There was, apparently, quite a commotion. I wasn't there myself, but it's not like the old man speaks to me much any more. Not that he ever did."

"You know Dubois personally?"

Sophie let out a deep sigh. "There were always… problems. He was a good friend of my father's. They spent a lot of time together when I was young, and I always heard about some of the crazy things he would spend his money on. He would throw his savings away on fast cars, lavish trips abroad, expensive paintings – it was like he couldn't control himself. A government salary is generous, but it doesn't begin to cover his tastes. There must have been a lot of debt. But for all his faults, he was not a bad man. He was not unkind."

"Do you think he had enough of a motive to steal museum property?" asked Leopold.

"I don't know. Even if he did steal something, how would he sell it? He would need some connections. He's not the kind of man who deals with criminals."

"Perhaps something pushed him over the edge?"

"Anything is possible. I'm sure he's made enough enemies over the years… but to steal from the museum? *Je ne sais pas*. It seems incredible to think about him in this way. Will you excuse me please?"

Leopold nodded as Sophie got to her feet and made her way through the door at the other end of the room, leaving the two men alone on the sofa.

"You've got that look," said Jerome, frowning.

"What look?"

"The look that tells me you're about to open up a giant can of worms and ruin a perfectly good vacation."

"You've got to admit," said Leopold, finishing his lemonade, "if Director Dubois was being kicked off the board, that does give him motive. Not just in terms of monetary gain, but revenge too. It's a powerful incentive."

"He would have had opportunity, too. But if there's one thing I've learned from our time together, we're not going to get very far without some inside information."

"Which is exactly why we need her," he jabbed a finger at the closed door. "She knows something she's not telling us."

Before Jerome could answer, Leopold's cell phone buzzed in his pocket. He fished out the handset and answered.

"I am speaking to Leopold Blake," the gruff voice on the line announced, more of a statement than a question.

"Yes. Who is this?"

"This is *Capitaine* Anton Rousseau with the *Préfecture de police de Paris*."

Leopold slapped his hand over the cell's microphone. "It's the police," he whispered to Jerome. "The museum must have reported the theft." He lifted the phone back to his ear. "Yes, *Capitaine*, I was expecting your call. How can I help?"

"You were expecting me?" Rousseau sounded surprised. "I understand you attempted to call *Monsieur* Dubois earlier today. You were the last telephone number registered on his telephone's memory. I need to speak with you urgently. Can you come down to my office?"

"I'm in the middle of an interview right now."

"I'm afraid I must insist."

"What's this all about, *Capitaine*?" asked Leopold, sensing he was missing something.

"I'm sorry to tell you this, *Monsieur* Blake, but Jean Dubois was murdered this afternoon. As you appear to be the last person to speak with him, I need to see you immediately."

TEN

The guttural hum of engine noise resonated throughout the decks of The *Thanatos*, a constant reminder to the crew that they were always on the move. Despite the thick insulation and maze of interior walls, Senior Operative James Cullen could tell the captain had just increased their speed.

"Wherever we're going, someone's in a hurry," said Rose, leaning in over his shoulder to get a better look at the monitors. "I've not had any alerts come through. Any idea where we're headed?"

"Not a clue," replied Cullen, scrolling through a text document. "Though it's hardly the Director's habit to keep people like us informed." He highlighted a block of text.

"Anything good?"

"Another Blake reference. Like the others, it's encrypted. But whatever it is, it's important enough for the Director to have everything sent to his personal feed."

"He's the one getting the updates?"

"Yeah. Though I can't see what's so important about this Blake guy." Cullen rested his chin in his hands.

"Who is he?"

"A nobody, really – just some guy with a trust fund. According to this," he opened up another document, "he inherited his parents' group of companies after they were killed in a hiking accident several years ago. Hardly surprising, given the weather conditions." He brought up a high-resolution image of the Khumbu Icefall, a treacherous stretch of terrain along the hiking trails leading up to Mount Everest.

"Robert and Giselle Blake owned the majority shareholding in Blake Investments Inc.," he continued, "which is an umbrella corporation for about a dozen other companies ranging from pharmaceutical and banking operations to military contractors and biological research. And pretty much everything else in between."

"So the guy's loaded?" asked Rose. "Maybe he's a possible source of funds."

Cullen shook his head. "Not likely. The Organization doesn't take money direct. They've got a whole division set up to handle that sort of thing. This must be about something else, otherwise the Director wouldn't be so interested. I guess they've got their eye on Blake for some other reason."

Rose chuckled. "We could always ask the Director what's going on. I hear he's great when it comes to sharing." She punched him playfully in the arm.

"Sure, why not," said James, grinning. "He loves it when his staff asks questions." He flipped back to the original encrypted document and sighed, scrolling through the reams of indecipherable text.

"Seriously though," Rose rested a hand on his shoulder. "What happens if we get caught looking at

this stuff? I've heard things... probably just rumors, but
—"

"I've covered our tracks, don't worry." He glanced up
into her eyes and registered a flash of concern. "They're
only rumors. Try to relax a little."

"You gotta admit, the guy's a little freaky," she added,
a wry smile returning to her lips. "I don't think I've
seen the Director outside of the bridge since I started
my rotation here, and that was six months ago. Does he
ever go outside?"

"Not that I know of. I guess he's got everything he
needs in there, and he's not exactly the sociable type."

"There's something about him that gives me the
creeps. Did you notice the scars?"

"Yeah, of course."

"Plastic surgery?"

Cullen shrugged. "Who knows. It doesn't pay to ask
questions. Which reminds me," he swiveled in his chair,
"don't breathe a word of this to anyone. It's not worth
our jobs to get busted on this. I'm tempted to just call
the whole thing off right now."

"What, and give up getting to spend time alone with
me?" said Rose, making pouty shapes with her lips.

"Please, don't tempt me," said James, giving her a
gentle shove. "Getting rid of you would be reward
enough."

"Aww, be nice," she replied. "I gotta go anyway.
Catch ya later, boss." She pecked him on the cheek.

"Get outta here, trouble."

Rose turned and strolled out of Cullen's office into
the hurly burly of the command center outside, leaving
the senior operative alone at his desk. With the privacy
glass set to full strength, the walls were a dull haze of

white light. Turning back to his computer screens, Cullen let out a deep sigh. With everything going on, he couldn't shake the feeling that he was getting in over his head.

ELEVEN

"What are you talking about? Who are you people?" Sophie's voice was strained, despite Leopold's attempts to break the news about Dubois' death to her gently. He stood, not really knowing what to do with his hands as he tried to comfort her, keenly aware that any pretense he had managed to forge was disintegrating around him.

"Who are you?" she repeated.

"We lied to you, Mlle. Bardot," he said. "We were working with M. Dubois to recover the stolen painting. Obviously, things have changed since we arrived. It was never our intention to cause trouble, we only want to do what's best for the museum."

"And I was a suspect?"

"We were just following a lead. In light of what's happened…" he tried to find the right words. "I think it's time we rethink things. I'm afraid we have to report to the police station downtown, I assume we'll need to give a statement. I can arrange to meet you later if –"

"Like hell you will," Sophie interrupted. "I've known Jean for twenty years. I'm coming with you." She grabbed a thin jacket from a hook on the wall and threw it on, as though daring anyone to convince her otherwise. "We can take my car. If anyone tries to talk me out of this, you can walk. *Comprenez-vous?*"

Leopold nodded. "We understand. I know this must be difficult for you."

"You don't understand anything. Have you ever had a loved one murdered?"

Jerome glanced at his employer.

"It's complicated," Leopold said. "I'm sure your car will be fine. Please," he gestured toward the doorway.

With a cold look, Sophie brushed past and set off toward the stairs. "The door will lock behind you."

Once outside, she pulled a set of keys from her purse and marched up to a battered blue Citroen 2CV that was parked a little way down the street. The wheel arches were peppered with rust and some of the paint had blistered in the sun, but it looked structurally sound despite being more than twenty years past its prime. Assuming it ever had one.

"This is your car?" asked Jerome, eyeing the cramped seats.

"Yes. You have a problem?" said Sophie, unlocking the doors and jostling the driver's side handle. "You'll struggle to find a taxi at this time of day."

The bodyguard didn't reply, settling himself into the back seat and buckling the seatbelt around his bulky frame as best he could.

"There's no problem," said Leopold. "Do you know the way?"

"Of course I know the way; I've lived in this city all my life. Maybe you can just be quiet until we arrive, okay?"

Nodding, Leopold fastened his own safety belt as Sophie started the car, which spluttered into life with a reluctant rattle from its twin cylinder engine. Nudging the vehicle to the brow of the hill, she pressed her foot to the clutch and coasted the car down the steep slope toward the main road out of Montmartre. As they merged with the traffic, Leopold couldn't shake the feeling that his vacation had come to a very sudden end.

TWELVE

The Paris police *Commisariat Central* headquarters were located south of the river, opposite the imposing Fontaine Saint-Sulpice, a dominating stone fountain incorporating four ornate statues depicting famous religious figures from history. The impressive monument rested upon four thick octagonal basins, concentric pedestals ringed with intricately carved stone lions that glared menacingly out over the city as cascades of water fell across their backs. In the shade of the great fountain, tourists and office workers sat and enjoyed the view, soaking up a little oasis of calm in the otherwise bustling neighborhood.

With a reluctant groan from the Citroen's rusty brake pads, Sophie rolled the car into an empty loading bay and killed the engine, which Leopold presumed was to prevent it from committing suicide. The heat inside the vehicle was unbearable thanks to the steel chassis and lack of air conditioning, and Leopold could feel the sweat on his brow.

"You're parking here?" asked Jerome from the back seat. "This is a loading zone. Won't you get a ticket?"

Sophie opened the driver's side door. "The worst they can do if I don't pay the ticket is impound the car, and this particular model is worth less than it would cost me to pay the fine. I can always get a new car."

The bodyguard shrugged and wrenched his own door open. "Suit yourself."

Without bothering to lock the car, Sophie led the way to the front of the building where a tall archway announced the main entrance. Feeling a wave of relief as the air conditioning blew a cold draft of air over his face, Leopold followed Sophie toward the reception area where the art restorer mumbled something to the middle aged woman manning the desk.

"She says to wait here," said Sophie, taking a seat close to the doors. "*Capitaine* Rousseau will come and collect us soon."

Obliging, Leopold sat down in silence next to her, catching the faint murmurs of some Europop chart-topper playing in the background. Sophie's eyes were focused on the far wall, deliberately avoiding him, and her legs were crossed – the body language alternative to "screw you."

"I didn't get a chance to say this before," said Leopold, trying to catch Sophie's attention, "but I'm sorry about how this turned out. We approached you as a suspect, and that was the wrong thing to do. If there's anything either of us can do…"

She turned to look at him. "You've done enough. Tell the police everything you know so that they can get to the bottom of this and find Jean's killer. Jean was a good man, but desperation can make people do very stupid things. Things that can get them killed." She bit her lip. "Let's just get out of here as soon as we can."

Leopold heard a door open and turned to see a tall, middle-aged man step into the room. He wore plain clothes, a dark shirt and jeans, and his silver hair was closely cropped in defiance of a receding hairline.

"*Bonjour*, I am *Capitaine* Rousseau," he announced in a thick accent. "Please, come with me." He waved them forward.

"Time to get this over with," said Leopold, getting to his feet. The others followed suit.

"Wait, who are you?" he aimed the question at Sophie.

"Sophie Bardot," she replied. "Old family friend of Jean Dubois."

"You are with these two?"

"I was with them when you called, *oui*."

"Then you can probably answer some questions, too. Follow me please."

Leopold struggled to keep pace with the policeman's long strides as he led them down a long, windowless corridor that smelled like cheap furniture polish.

"I recognize him," Sophie whispered, leaning in to Leopold's ear. "He's been on television. Something about a string of murders. They call him *Le Loup* – The Wolf – because he always tracks down his prey."

"That's a little melodramatic," Leopold whispered back.

Sophie shrugged. "I'm just saying, it looks like they've brought in the big guns. Whatever's going on, it must be making some very important people worried."

They rounded a corner and Rousseau stopped outside a scuffed wooden door. A plaque fastened to the front read *salle d'entrevue*.

"Please, go in and take a seat." He ushered them through.

In the center of the cramped room was a square table with four chairs. A tape recorder was bolted in place at elbow height, allowing the interviewer easy access to pause and rewind as needed. The room was brightly lit and there was a ubiquitous one-way mirror installed along the back wall. Leopold dragged one of the chairs around to the other side of the table, allowing him to sit opposite Rousseau with Sophie and Jerome at his side. Each took their seats and Rousseau began.

"Thank you for coming at such short notice," he said, rolling the words across his tongue. "And Mlle. Bardot, I am very sorry for your loss."

Sophie nodded, saying nothing.

"Mr. Blake, I must start by asking what you and M. Dubois discussed during your meeting earlier today. I took the liberty of calling the museum for his schedule. How were you two involved?"

Leopold considered his reply. "The Louvre hired me as a security consultant. It was a last minute arrangement. Dubois and I met today to discuss some of my initial recommendations."

"Which were?"

"I noticed some serious flaws in the systems they were using. I asked him to call a staff meeting."

"What time was this?"

"Around twelve-thirty."

"And Dubois stayed for the meeting?"

"No, he left shortly after I began."

Rousseau leaned forward. "And then?"

"The staff meeting lasted about thirty minutes. After that, we spoke with H.R. and went to see Mlle. Bardot."

"When did you meet her?"

"Around two P.M."

"Do you have anything that shows where you were for the time between the staff meeting and speaking with Mlle. Bardot?"

"No. We took a cab and paid cash."

"No receipt?"

Leopold's eyes narrowed. "I didn't think we'd need one."

"I spoke with an employee at the museum who says that you and M. Dubois were arguing shortly before he left the museum. The witness also says…" he pulled a folded piece of notepaper out of his pocket and studied it carefully. "He says that you were tied to a chair? *Mon Dieu*, why would he do this?"

"You know how it is; sometimes people don't like it when outsiders tell them how to do their jobs. We had a minor disagreement. He quickly saw things from my point of view. There was no issue."

"Of course, it happens all the time for me, too." He smiled, a warm grin that creased up the skin around his eyes. "And who was it that hired you? Was it Dubois himself?"

"No. I get the impression he wanted to use someone local, but his bosses overruled him."

"So Dubois was not kept in the loop? I suppose this is normal for a man close to retirement. I only hope they give me a little more warning when my time comes." He smiled again.

"I suppose," said Leopold. "So, are we going to talk about what happened? Perhaps if we knew a little more about how… about the circumstances. It might help."

"Of course, of course," Rousseau said, drumming his fingers on the table. "Tell me," he directed his question at Jerome, "what kind of bullet could cause enough damage to punch through six inches of concrete wall?"

The bodyguard's eyes narrowed. "I'm sure there are hundreds of possibilities."

"You have military training, don't you Jerome? I apologize for my rudeness, but I couldn't find any mention of your surname. But you have served with the military, *non?*"

"Yes."

"And you work in private security now."

"Yes."

Rousseau appeared to consider his next words carefully. "And Mr. Blake, you can certainly afford the best, isn't that true?"

"You've spent time researching us, I see," said Leopold.

"Of course."

"Then you're aware I can have a senior partner from any top law firm in the city here within thirty minutes. I would choose my questions wisely, if I were you, *Capitaine.*"

"*Je suis désolé* – I am sorry, forgive my rudeness. Yes, I looked you up; I do so for anyone I interview. I believe you inherited quite the windfall after your parents' deaths. It must have been a very difficult time."

"I've dealt with worse."

"You must have made some very strong connections in France after you opened your offices here, *non?*"

"I wasn't involved in the La Defense projects, but I understand they all went smoothly."

"Yes, yes. Very smoothly. It is quite unusual for construction deals to complete quite so quickly, especially in La Defense. You must have quite the influence, Mr. Blake."

Leopold didn't reply.

"And Mlle. Bardot," Rousseau continued, looking over at Sophie, "you first met these gentlemen this afternoon?"

"*Oui*, they told me they were from an art magazine and needed an interview for an upcoming article. After I let them in the house, they revealed they were working with Jean... with M. Dubois. Then you called. So, here I am."

"And you have never met them before today?"

"No."

"And you were at home all day, until now?"

"Yes. You can check my phone records if you like. I made a call around lunchtime from my landline."

"*Oui*, I know," smiled Rousseau. "I already checked. Thank you for your help." He turned back to Leopold. "You were not forthcoming with her?"

"It helps to interview possible leads when they don't know what's going on," replied Leopold. "It keeps them off guard. But you should know this."

"Indeed I do, indeed I do." The police captain sat back and sucked in a deep breath. "I will tell you what happened to M. Dubois. I apologize, Mlle. Bardot, if this upsets you."

"Just tell me," she said. "It's better than not knowing."

"A few minutes after one P.M. this afternoon, Jean Dubois and four other people were killed near the Notre Dame plaza, just outside the steps that lead up from the metro station. It appears that the killer targeted M. Dubois first and then proceeded to open fire at other people on the street. This helped to create confusion and allowed him to get away. He used a high caliber rife round, a .338, and was positioned at the top of one of the cathedral's towers. We also found the body of a police constable who appears to have attempted to prevent his escape."

"Do you have any leads?" asked Sophie, her eyes welling.

"*Oui*, I have some. I am working hard on them right now," said Rousseau. "Some very strong leads."

"I think it's time we were going," said Leopold, getting to his feet. "We've done all we can to help. I wish you luck, *Capitaine*."

"Before you go, can you help me with something?" asked the police captain. "Perhaps you can shed some light on this?" He reached into his pocket and retrieved a second sheet of folded paper, unfolding it face up on the tabletop.

Leopold noticed a smudgy black image. "A fingerprint?"

"Not just any fingerprint," said Rousseau. "This is your fingerprint, Mr. Blake. We found this at the cathedral, in the exact spot the shooter used. Would you care to explain how it got there?"

The consultant frowned. "If I knew how it got there, I would have brought my lawyer with me. I suppose there was no other evidence to be found?"

"Not a trace. It seems you got sloppy with cleaning up after yourself."

"This is insane," said Leopold, glancing at Sophie. She was staring at him, dumbfounded. "I had nothing to do with this. Someone obviously wants me to take the blame."

"And I assume you can prove otherwise?" said Rousseau.

"It's not up to me to prove my innocence, *Capitaine*. You'll need something a little more conclusive than a smudged fingerprint."

"Understood, understood. But this is how I see it: I have two foreigners," he gestured at Leopold and Jerome, "who arrive in France days before the murder. One of the foreigners is military trained and an expert in firearms, having practised in private security for the last twenty years. The other foreigner has a very public argument with the director, just minutes before he is shot, about some mysterious security system issue. I have enough to secure a formal charge against you, at the very least. Perhaps a judge will feel differently, but I can't very well let you leave, can I? Not with all your resources. You will have to stay here until we can arrange a court hearing."

"I'm afraid that's out of the question," said Leopold. "We need to be leaving now."

"That will not be possible. I'm arresting you, both of you, for conspiracy to commit murder. You have the right to assistance from a lawyer. If you cannot afford a lawyer, we will provide one for you. You have the right to remain silent under questioning, although failure to answer questions –"

"Yes, yes, I know the drill," said Leopold. "I can waive reading of my rights, thank you. Are we done here?"

"I'm very sorry to tell you, Mr. Blake," said Rousseau, making his way to the door, "but this is really only just beginning."

THIRTEEN

Mary Jordan rolled her hastily-packed suitcase through the Charles De Gaulle airport customs area and tried not to make eye contact with the security staff. Head down, she passed through the checkpoint without incident and joined the flow of traffic toward the arrivals lounge, heading straight for the nearest coffee place once she hit the lobby. After nearly eight hours stuffed into cattle-class, a decent cup of coffee was pretty much the only thing on the planet that had any chance of keeping her upright. Spotting an empty table at a nearby Starbucks, she headed for the counter at a brisk pace, hoping to get her order in before someone else got the same idea.

She picked up her drink and nestled herself at the table. Grimacing as the taste of burnt coffee beans coated her tongue, Mary remembered why most people don't stick around for airport refreshments. *Still, caffeine is caffeine*, she reasoned, taking another slurp. Pulling out her cell phone, she turned the handset on and waited for it to pick up a local signal. Having forked out fifty bucks for a weeks' worth of roaming charges, now was as good a time as any to catch up on her email.

The cell phone buzzed excitedly as the screen sprang into life, announcing seven missed calls and three voicemails. All from the same number. With a resigned sigh, Mary dialed her mom and held the phone up to her ear, experience suggesting that getting this conversation out of the way would save a heap of trouble later on. After a few rings, her mother answered.

"Hello? Hello? Who's this?"

"Relax mom," said Mary, tipping the remainder of the bitter espresso down her neck. "It's me. What's so important you needed to get through to me over the Atlantic?"

"Oh, I'm sorry hon. You know I don't know how to use these damn things. I must have redialed you or something, I was trying to send out a chirp... is that the right word? That little birdy thing you put on here for me?"

"You mean Twitter?"

"Yeah, that's the one. I was trying to send a Twitter. Anyway, how was the flight? You land okay?"

"Sure, mom. Look, if you're busy, I could really –"

"No, no. I'm glad you called back, honey. I didn't want to bring it up this morning, what with you rushing out and all, but I do need to speak with you about something really important. Have you got time?"

Mary checked her watch. "I'm supposed to be getting picked up right about now. But I guess he won't mind if I'm a few minutes late. What's up?"

"Well, I know it's been a few years, but your sister's been in touch."

Mary's heart caught in her chest.

"Honey? You there?"

"Yeah, mom. I'm here. I just haven't thought about her in a while."

"I know sweetie. It's been hard for all of us, but... well, I told her I'd mention it to you and see –"

"And see if I can bring myself to speak to her again?" Mary interrupted. "After what she did, I don't know why you just didn't hang up the phone right there and then."

"She's my daughter too, sweetie. I never stopped caring about her."

"And you want me to talk to her?"

"Just *think* about it, okay? I'm not saying everything's forgiven, but... well, I miss her! And I miss you two getting along. It's not right that two sisters haven't spoken with each other in five years. Just not natural."

Mary sighed. "I'll think about it, mom. But no promises."

"That's my girl."

"Listen, I've got to go, I'm running late."

"Okay, hon. Love you."

"You too." Mary heard the line go dead.

Feeling the caffeine start to take hold, she got to her feet and gathered up her suitcase, glancing around for instructions on where to find the pickup zone. After ten minutes peering at her cell phone's translation software, she drummed up the courage to ask one of the airport concierges for help. Directed toward the far end of the building, Mary found the exit that led out onto the main concourse, where a rabble of jet-lagged passengers stood waiting for taxis. It was nearly nine P.M. but the sun was still shining and there was at least an hour of daylight left, meaning plenty of opportunity to get into the city and find a nice terrace bar, have a few drinks, and get something to eat. She glanced around for her ride, but could only make out a long line of cabs.

Pulling out her cell phone, Mary dialed a number from memory and waited for the call to go through. She was greeted by a pre-recorded message.

"This is Leopold Blake. Please leave a voicemail."

Dammit. She made a mental note to make him pay for dinner. She made another mental note to make sure she ordered the most expensive thing on the menu. Slipping the handset back into her pocket, Mary glanced around and wondered how long she'd have to wait before giving up and getting a taxi.

In the distance, she noticed the rows of hotel blocks just beyond the outer perimeter of the airport and wondered whether it might just be easier to grab a room and hope for better luck in the morning. Squinting at the closest building, Mary could make out a slight glimmer on the otherwise featureless roof – a tiny pinprick of light that was just bright enough to draw her attention.

FOURTEEN

Reiniger peered through the rifle scope and lined up his shot. Having swapped out the barrel and changed ammunition, even if the police did recover the round they wouldn't be able to match it with the earlier targets, which would keep them guessing long enough for him to complete the mission.

He lay on his stomach atop the Charles De Gaulle Hilton Hotel, a little over one thousand meters away from his target and well within the rifle's effective range. The wind had picked up considerably since Notre Dame and the airport forecourt was a lot busier than he had anticipated, which was an added challenge he could do without. Still, he had made much more difficult kills, so this should be a walk in the park. Concentrating, he watched his target closely and felt himself fall into sync with her movements, just as he had done countless times before.

Just a little further, he willed his target to take a few steps forward, away from the steel railings that blocked a clear shot to her chest. Reiniger briefly considered switching positions to get a better angle before noticing the woman was looking straight at him. His eyes seemed to meet hers. The assassin's finger brushed against the trigger, ready to fire. His pulse quickened, momentarily.

A gust of cool air whipped past his head, ruffling his hair and whistling through his ears. The wind speed felt like at least twelve knots, which meant a head shot was out of the question. She would have to venture away from the relative safety of the taxi shelter to allow a clear shot to the torso.

Just a little further. Through the scope, Reiniger watched a bus pull up, blocking his view. He saw the doors slide open and a rabble of elderly holidaymakers pour out onto the asphalt, dragging their hand luggage behind them. The driver rushed ahead, pulling open the baggage compartments at the side, heaving suitcases out on to the forecourt.

The assassin swore, his profanities lost in the wind. Earlier in the week he had spent the best part of a day staking out the airport's numerous pick up zones, and not once had a tour bus ventured anywhere near. This particular driver must have gotten lost somewhere in the maze of one way systems and given up, presumably eager to unload and move on to the next job.

Goddamn amateurs.

A moment later his suspicions were confirmed as he saw an irate airport official march toward the huddle of pensioners with a walkie-talkie pressed to his lips. He and the bus driver proceeded to argue, their arms flailing. The assassin couldn't tell what they were saying, but the body language was universal and neither seemed in any rush to back down.

Unexpected wind speed. Unexpected obstacles. A forecourt full of witnesses. If Reiniger had learned anything from his long and brutal career, it was that uncertainty leads to mistakes. And mistakes lead to getting caught. Or killed. More often than not, a simple twist of fate could make all the difference between a successful job and a botched one, and this was one mission that had to go off without a hitch.

Frowning, the assassin adjusted the lens and zoomed in, right up to the maximum possible setting. Through the bus' windows, he could still make out his target; she was on the move, heading straight for the line of waiting taxis. He watched her pull her police badge from her pocket and wave it in front of her as she walked, mouthing something he couldn't make out. The line of people moved out of her way as she made a bee line for the nearest cab. He made a mental note of the license plate as she climbed inside.

Taking his eye from the scope, Reiniger took a moment to consider his options. This was not necessarily a reason to abort. He knew where the target was headed, and could make a pretty good idea what she would do once she found out why her ride hadn't showed. There was only one building in Paris where she would go and Reiniger already knew the layout. It would be simple enough to wait for her to come to him. Instead of risking a tricky shot from long range, he now had the opportunity to indulge in a more intimate approach, something up close and personal.

Yes, this could work out very well indeed.

With excitement welling up inside him, Reiniger quickly disassembled the rifle and packed it back into the carry case. Pulling out the KA-BAR knife, he checked the edge against his thumb and suppressed a grin.

Very well indeed.

FIFTEEN

"How much longer?"

Leopold had resisted the urge to shout for the guards, but Sophie's tireless questioning was beginning to grate. For the last few hours, he and Jerome had been locked in a holding cell and after almost thirty minutes of arguing, Sophie had convinced Captain Rousseau to let her sit with them. Leopold was regretting that decision already. She was now sat on a wooden stool, watching the two men through the steel bars that separated her from the tiny cell. Jerome lay serenely on the bed, while Leopold paced the floor in irritation.

"We'll be in here until they can move us over to the main prison," he said. "Which should be in the next couple of hours. Only a judge can grant us bail at this point, and I doubt Rousseau's in any hurry to get the paperwork done."

"I thought you had connections?" said Sophie. "Isn't there anything you can do?"

"My lawyer can suppress anything said during the interview, up until the point where Rousseau officially arrested us. Like he said, I've got a right to a lawyer, but I can't force them to rush the process. They haven't even given me a phone call yet."

"Okay, okay, don't get upset. I can make a call for you, as soon as I go back outside. What do I tell your lawyer?"

"You tell them to send someone down here immediately. Call Cotty, Vivant, Marchisio & Lauzeral – tell them I'll only need them to handle the transfer. I'll get my usual defense attorney on an airplane when I get a chance, and he can handle the difficult stuff."

"Why did they charge you with *conspiracy* to murder?" she asked.

Leopold smiled. "It's a fallback position for the prosecutor. Believe me, whoever planted that evidence at the scene isn't going to keep me off the streets for long. You can count on it."

"Still, until then you're stuck in here. I believed you when you said you had nothing to do with Jean, but… *Je ne sais pas,* I don't know."

"What is it?" Leopold looked at Sophie. For the first time, he sensed something else underneath her cool exterior. Fear.

"Someone planned this. If Jean was mixed up in all this, now I am too. God only knows what they have planned for me."

"But that doesn't –"

"You have to get out of here," she grabbed hold of the steel bars with both hands. "Do whatever it takes. They've killed people already, they won't think twice about coming after me. Who's to say they aren't already waiting outside? Or at my apartment? I can't survive without help."

He held her gaze. "I'll be in here a couple of days, that's all. Is there somewhere you can go?"

"They'll send people after me, don't you see? What kind of chance do I have? There must be something you can do."

"Mary." Jerome sat up. "Mary was due to land an hour ago. You were supposed to pick her up. If Mlle. Bardot is right, she could be in danger too."

"Sophie, I need you to call someone for me," said Leopold. "A friend of mine called Mary Jordan. She's a cop."

"And what about me? What am I supposed to do?"

"She can help."

"Fine. Give me the number."

Leopold recited the number from memory. Sophie nodded and made her way to the exit. She knocked on the door and the guard let her through.

"I suppose you've got a plan," said Leopold, turning to face Jerome.

"Don't worry about that," he said, lying back on the mattress. "Worry about the guys that did this to us."

"And if we can't find Mary?"

The bodyguard smiled. "Then we're going to have to get out of here a hell of a lot sooner than we planned."

SIXTEEN

"He's been what?" Sat in the back of the taxi, Mary pressed her cell phone to her ear and tried to concentrate.

"Ma'am, I checked the report myself."

"Call me *ma'am* again and you'll be sorry, Detective," replied Mary.

"Sorry m – I mean, sorry, Sergeant Jordan."

"Read it out for me again. Your signal's breaking up a little."

"Yeah, sure. I ran Blake's name through the Interpol database over here in New York. I got quite a few hits, but the one that stood out was an arrest registered today, just a few hours ago. In Paris, France."

Mary sighed. "I was afraid I'd heard you right the first time. Where's he being held?"

"Gimme a minute."

The taxi sped up a little and Mary turned to look out the back window. She spotted a black VW Passat just two vehicles behind her, keeping its distance. The car had followed them ever since they left the airport.

"You still there?"

Mary snapped out of her thoughts. "Yeah, what you got for me?"

"He's being held at…" the detective paused. "Erm, the *Commisariat Central* police headquarters just a little south of the river. I'll text you the address."

"Thanks. Listen, can you do me one more favor?"

"Whatever you need."

"Can you run me a license plate?" She turned to look out the rear window again. "Keep it quiet, though. I just need to check something out."

"No problem, Sarge."

"Thanks, I owe you one. Can you run it now?"

"Yeah, shouldn't take a minute. What's the number?"

"Hang on." She leaned forward to speak to the taxi driver. "Hey, you speak English?"

The cabbie grunted. "*Un peu.*"

"I need you to move into the other lane."

"*Porquoi?* Why? This is the fastest lane."

"Just do it."

The driver muttered something incomprehensible and moved over, letting the traffic stream ahead on the left. The black VW cruised past and Mary read out the license plate.

"Okay, got it," said the detective. "Anything else?"

"No that's it; just run the number for me."

"Sure. Just let me put you on hold a few minutes."

"No, don't put –" she began, but the Muzak had already started. Switching the headset into speaker mode, she dropped the phone on to her lap and tried to think about something else.

This was Mary's first vacation in years, but it was already starting to feel like just another day in the office. And not a good day, either. On reflection, she was beginning to regret getting out of bed already.

SEVENTEEN

"I couldn't get through," said Sophie, walking back into the holding room. "I'm sorry. Her phone is either turned off, or she's using it. I tried calling a few times, but no luck." She sat back down on the stool.

"She might be trying to track us down," said Leopold.

"Or someone got to her already," said Jerome, getting to his feet. "And unless you've got a genetically engineered clone running around shooting people, somebody's gone to a great deal of trouble to make sure you wound up in jail tonight. The only chance you got of getting out of here early was if Mary pulled some strings with the local P.D. and got you a bail hearing. You think whoever's behind this is going to take that chance? We need to make a move. Now."

Sophie fidgeted and looked toward the door. "And how do you expect to get out of here?"

"Leave that to us," said Jerome.

"Sophie, we'll need your help," said Leopold.

"Me?"

"It's the only way we're going to pull this off. Otherwise, they ship us off to the prison and God only knows what could be waiting for us there."

Sophie sighed. "What do I have to do?"

Leopold leaned in closer. "Make enough noise to get those three guards in here, and we'll do the rest."

"Make enough noise?"

"You'll know what I mean when it's time." He turned back to Jerome. "You ready?"

"Ready." Jerome smiled and shoved both his giant hands into Leopold's chest, throwing him against the steel bars. As the consultant crumpled to the floor, Jerome grabbed his collar and threw him onto the bed.

"This would be the part where you make a little noise, if you wouldn't mind?" said Jerome, wrapping both hands around Leopold's neck. "As much as I'm enjoying myself, I don't think he's going to last long."

"You're hurting him!"

"It needs to look authentic for the cameras. Just make some noise."

"Okay, okay." Sophie took a deep breath and let out a scream.

After five long seconds, the holding room door burst open and three guards stormed inside, shoving Sophie out of the way. The shortest of the officers fumbled with a set of keys before finally wrenching the metal gate open, sliding the bars to the side.

"*Arretez!*" he shouted, raising his baton above his head as he and the others stepped into the cell.

Jerome shook Leopold violently and drew back his fist. The three guards panicked and rushed forward, the shorter one grabbing hold of the bodyguard's thick forearm while the others stood ready at the rear.

Jerome moved fast, kicking the shorter man in the stomach and wrenching the baton from his hand. The guard sailed backward into one of his companions, sending them both tumbling to the ground. The remaining officer froze, clearly unsure of how to react without his partners backing him up. Without waiting for an invitation, Jerome stepped forward and landed a roundhouse punch to the guard's jaw, knocking him down with an unceremonious grunt.

"Move, now!" said Jerome, stepping over the pile of incapacitated police officers.

"Quick, this way." Sophie waved them forward, holding the door open.

"We've got less than thirty seconds before they figure out what's happened and sound the alarm. You get the keys?"

Leopold nodded, unhooking a keychain from one of the guard's belts. "We'd better hope one of these works."

"No time for second thoughts now," said Jerome, stepping through into the corridor. "Twenty-five seconds. Keep up."

The trio bounded down the hallway toward the door at the end and Leopold fumbled at the handle. Locked. He fished out the key ring and stared blankly at the dozen metal keys before giving up and selecting one at random.

"Fifteen seconds," said Jerome.

"Okay, okay, I get it. Just let me try this one." The key didn't even fit in the hole. He tried another. "No good. Hang on."

"Ten seconds."

"Thanks for the reminder." He rattled a third key without success. "You've got to be kidding."

"Five."

"Hang on…"

"Four."

"This one's going to work…"

"Three, two…"

"Okay, maybe the next –"

"One."

"Oh *mon Dieu*, just give them to me," said Sophie. She slipped one of the keys into the lock and twisted. The door opened with a satisfying *clunk*. "After you, gentlemen."

"That was the one I was going for next," muttered Leopold. As he stepped through, the piercing sound of alarm bells filled the corridor.

"Looks like the security boys have finally caught up," said Jerome, breaking into a jog. "Follow me."

The bodyguard led them down the hallway, toward the exit doors at the far end. "The doors out to the street will be sealed by now," he said. "If we can make it to the roof, there's a chance we can find a way onto the next building. Or maybe a fire escape."

"What did he just say?" asked Sophie, quickening her pace. "The roof?"

"If you've got any better ideas, now's the time." Jerome reached the exit and burst through without breaking his stride.

Two police officers rounded the corner ahead and barreled towards them, batons raised. Jerome lowered his shoulders, just as the officer in front drew back his weapon. Grabbing the man's forearm, he pivoted and threw the policeman over his shoulder, thrusting out his elbow and catching the other officer in the temple, toppling him to the ground. He snatched both officers' radios and tossed them into a garbage can.

"Are you done showing off?" said Leopold. "We need to get to the roof before this whole place is swarming."

"How do you know where we're going?" asked Sophie. "What are we looking for?"

"It's a combination of brains and luck," said Leopold. "And the fact that the stairwell is clearly marked probably helps, too." He pointed to a sign at the end of the hallway. "Keep moving."

The next door opened out into a junction, connecting several corridors into a central T-junction. Glancing around, Leopold spotted the stairs that led up to the roof. A metal bar across the front instead of a handle was marked *Pousser Pour Ouvrir*.

"Wait," said Jerome. "If the door's alarmed, they'll know where we're headed."

"We don't have a choice," said Leopold. "If we spend any more time looking for another way up, they'll overwhelm us."

"I don't think that's going to matter much soon," said Sophie. "Listen."

Leopold heard heavy footsteps approaching from somewhere along one of the corridors.

"Sounds like we've got company," said Jerome. "You ready to move?"

They both nodded.

"Then go. I'll hold them off as long as I can."

"You'll what?" said Leopold.

"The only way you're walking away from this is if I can buy you some time. I can hold them off while you make it onto the roof. Hopefully, I'll be able to stay on my feet long enough for you to find a way out of here."

"You'll be outnumbered."

"Won't be the first time."

"You've never had to deal with a building full of pissed-off cops before."

"I'll be waiting for them in the stairwell. Their numbers won't count for much if they've got to come at me one by one." He fixed his gaze on Leopold. "You have to go. Now. It's the only way."

Somewhere ahead, the sound of footsteps grew louder.

"You have to come with us."

"This isn't a negotiation. You need to figure out what's going on, otherwise, we're both going down. Permanently."

Leopold saw the intensity in Jerome's eyes and realized the futility of arguing. "Whoever's behind this will have people waiting at the prison, you know that."

"Let me worry about that. I can look after myself."

"I know. Just make sure you don't do anything stupid, okay?"

"Too late for that." Jerome smiled. "I agreed to take this trip, didn't I?"

Leopold managed a weak grin in reply. He grabbed hold of Sophie's wrist once again and shoved the door open, setting off another alarm just as a stream of uniformed police officers charged around the corner.

"Go, I'll hold them off," said Jerome, backing through the door.

Leopold headed for the stairs and dragged Sophie behind. The narrow staircase was poorly lit and steep, zigzagging its way up to the roof. Glancing behind, he saw Jerome take up his position at the foot of the stairs, blocking the way.

"What are you waiting for?" Sophie hissed, tugging at his wrist. "We need to get out of here."

Leopold held his ground. Despite his old friend's orders, he couldn't just leave without making sure Jerome knew what he was doing. Fortunately, he needn't have worried.

As the first officer bounded through the doorway, Jerome thrust out a giant palm and struck the man in the nose, snapping his head back and throwing him into the wall. Another cop followed and a jab to the throat put him out of commission before he could take another step. A third officer pushed through, followed by a fourth, then a fifth, clambering over the bodies of their comrades. Their shouts were drowned out by the noise of the alarms.

Leopold could barely see Jerome any more, his view blocked by the rabble of policeman attempting to drive the bodyguard back. It was only a matter of time before they broke through and Leopold knew their freedom depended on making it to the roof before that happened. He felt Sophie pulling at his arm again and he turned to look at her, catching the fear and panic in her eyes.

"Okay, you win. Let's go." He bounded up the stairs, taking them two at a time, with Sophie not far behind. The climb to the top felt like an eternity, adrenaline making him feel as though he were moving in slow motion.

His heartbeat thumping in his ears, Leopold finally reached the summit and threw all his weight against the metal door blocking their path. It held fast.

"It's locked," said Sophie, catching her breath. "We're stuck. We should give ourselves up before someone gets hurt."

He lowered his shoulders and tried again. "No. It's not locked, just stiff. We keep moving." He grunted with the effort, slamming his body into the metal. The door began to give way as a barrage of shouts echoed up the stairwell.

"It's working! Let me help." She squeezed in next to him and pushed.

The door let out a metallic screech as the warped hinges began to give way. Leopold felt fresh air on his face as a crack of light appeared, their path to freedom tantalizingly close.

"Nearly there, keep going." Leopold grunted with the effort, his muscles straining.

With a final push, Sophie added an extra jolt and the door burst open. Stumbling through the doorway, the consultant froze. The roof was slanted and clad with smooth tiles, only a narrow strip separating them from a sixty foot plummet. The dwindling sunlight cast long shadows across the scene, making it almost impossible to make out a clear path.

"What are you waiting for?" Sophie hissed, forcing the door back into its frame. "We need to find a way out of here. That door won't hold them for long."

"One wrong move and we could slip right over the edge." He glanced out toward the precipice.

"So what do we do? Just wait here to get picked up?"

"No. Look over there." He pointed to the far side of the roof. "We're in a pretty old part of the city. Most of these buildings were designed to share essentials like gas and water. There should be some kind of access between the two."

"You're certain?"

"There's only one way to be sure." He grabbed hold of her hand. "Follow me." Leopold crept forward, his eyes scanning the surface in front of his feet for any signs of loose tiling or other trip hazards, but the lack of light was making progress slow and difficult.

"Can you hear that?" Sophie asked.

Tilting his head, Leopold caught the faint but unmistakable sound of sirens, lots of sirens. They were getting closer. "Someone must have called for reinforcements. Try to ignore it."

"Ignore it? Half of the Paris police department are about to show up, and I don't think –" A loud, metallic clang cut her off mid-sentence.

Leopold put his finger to his lips. "Sash. Keep quiet, and keep low."

The sound came again, a grinding and screeching of twisted metal.

"It sounds like they got past Jerome," said Leopold. "We're out of time."

EIGHTEEN

"Stop the car." Mary stared out of the back window of the cab as the vehicle slowed to a standstill. Her jaw dropped.

"*Madame*," the cabbie looked at her over his shoulder. "This is not a safe place to stop. You would rather I let you out around the corner?"

Mary didn't reply. The streets outside were teeming with police, most of whom were running in the direction of the *Commissariat Central* front doors. Three marked vehicles had formed a blockade across the main roads leading away from the station, their red and blue lights flashing. Yellow police tape stretched across the sidewalk, keeping the pedestrians at bay. A few armed officers had their weapons drawn and were stalking the perimeter of the building, dressed in full body armor. If Mary had been in any doubt that Leopold was nearby, all uncertainty now vanished.

Always desperate for attention. She fished a twenty Euro note from her purse and handed it to the driver. Stepping out onto the road, she shut the car door and the driver sped off. Narrowly avoiding a collision with a camera-wielding spectator, she dragged her luggage over to the sidewalk and found an empty seat near an impressive fountain. Ignoring the water splashing onto her shoes, she watched the chaos unfolding across the street.

As the sun set over the skyline, the street lamps flickered into life and cast long shadows across the sidewalk. Squinting at the dozens of prowling silhouettes, Mary pulled out her cell phone and noticed several missed call alerts. She didn't recognize the number, but made an executive decision and hit redial.

The call connected and someone picked up. The sound of strong wind at the other end crackled in the speaker, but Mary could just about make out a voice. A woman's voice, with a strong French accent.

"*Allô?* Is that Mary?"

"Who the hell is this?"

"Hang on."

Mary heard a scuffling sound and a familiar voice came on the line.

"You've caught me at a bad time, Mary."

"Leopold? What the hell are you doing? Where are you? What's with all the cops?"

"Like I said, this isn't the best time." There was a brief pause. "Are you nearby?"

"I'm at the fountain, looking straight at the police H.Q. You've made quite a mess, Leopold."

"Entirely necessary, I assure you. Long story short, we're up on the roof. Someone set me up and I need to get out of here. It's my only chance to figure out what's going on."

"This is the most —"

"We can talk about it later," Leopold interrupted. "Look, I need your help."

Mary resisted the urge to scream down the phone. "You need help?"

"If we can get across to the next building before they see us, the police will think we slipped out on one of the lower floors."

"So?"

"On the northeast corner of the building there's an alleyway. See it?"

Mary squinted. "What about it?"

"See the cop standing there?"

"The one with the submachine gun?"

"That's the one. I need you to distract him."

"Distract him? Why?"

"We can make it across the gap between the two buildings using the pipes that run along the walls, but I'll need you to keep the attention away from us for a few minutes. Can you do that?"

"Leopold, I –"

"Can you do it, Mary?"

She sighed. "Yes."

"Then get moving. We've got people trying to break a door down up here. Not to put you under pressure or anything."

"I'm on the way. Just make sure you get your ass down here so I can kick it back to New York, where it belongs."

"I knew you'd –"

She hung up the phone, cutting him off. She watched the armed police officer standing guard near the alleyway across the street. He stood with both hands on his weapon, glancing up and down the road. Apparently satisfied the escape routes were covered, he turned to survey the alleyway behind him.

Shit. Her phone still in her hand, Mary ditched her luggage and sprinted across the road, making a beeline for the armed policeman.

Don't look up, don't look up. Shit, shit, shit.

Mary summoned a final burst of strength and lengthened her stride. As she drew close, she let out a high-pitched squeal and fell to the ground, rolling unceremoniously into the nearby wall.

"Madame? Etes-vous blessé?"

Looking up from the floor, Mary saw the armed officer approach, one hand held out. She took it, and he helped her onto her feet.

"Que s'est-il passé?" he asked. His nametag read "Beaumont."

"I'm sorry, I don't speak French." Mary smiled and pushed back her hair. "Erm... *Parlez-vous Anglais?*"

Beaumont nodded. "Yes, English is fine. What are you doing here? This is a secure area. You need to step back."

"I was mugged. Someone stole my purse and now I've hurt my leg." She hobbled slightly to prove the point. "Can you help me? Please? I don't know what else to do. I'm here by myself and I don't know anyone. I just need a little help." She looked up and caught a glimpse of movement on the roof above. She quickly dropped her gaze. "Please?"

Beaumont's features softened slightly. "There's a medical team close by. I can get them to come. Can you walk?"

She hobbled slightly, but retained her balance. Stealing a brief glance into the shadows above, she noticed two figures shimmying their way slowly across the gap between the buildings.

"I – I don't know," she replied, wincing in mock pain. "Can you take me?"

"I can't leave my post."

"Maybe you could just... can you just help me stand? My leg hurts too much to walk."

"It's not safe for you here. If you could –" A scuffling noise cut him off and he turned his head to check behind him.

Mary felt her heart in her throat. Without stopping to think, she threw herself forward and wrapped both arms around Beaumont's waist. "I'm so sorry!" she spluttered, as he jerked in surprise. "I tripped! I can't stand up straight with this leg... Please, can you just help me over to the corner? I'm sure someone can take me from there."

Beaumont glared at her. "*Madame*, please take your hands off me."

"Look, just help me hobble over to the corner. I'm sure someone else can take me from there."

He paused. "Please, be quick. I can take you."

"Thank you, thank you. Erm... *Merci*." Mary smiled and took the officer's arm. He led her away from the alleyway and toward the huddle of cops at the street corner.

"Just make sure you stay out of the way," said Beaumont.

"Of course, no problem," said Mary. "I'm just having a really bad day, that's all."

NINETEEN

Peering through the Yukon Ranger Pro night vision scope, Dieter Reiniger contemplated the carnage unfolding in front of him. Sitting in the relative safety of his black VW two blocks from the *Commissariat Central*, the assassin could make out the action as though he were just a few feet away, all rendered in sharp focus through the high-resolution LCD display.

Blake and the French girl had somehow managed to escape onto the roof and across to the adjacent building, but the bodyguard was nowhere to be seen. Reiniger counted himself lucky for that small mercy. Mary Jordan had shown up, as expected, meaning she and Blake would attempt to regroup somewhere close by.

Reiniger lowered the monocular and took a deep breath. The building next to the police headquarters looked like a regular office complex, the perfect place for Blake and the others to rendezvous undetected. Thankfully, it was also the perfect place to put an end to this mess and get the mission back on track. There was still time.

Stowing the scope in the glove box, the assassin swung open the driver's door and stepped out into the street, resting his hand against the gun holstered beneath his jacket. Making his way toward the chaos ahead, he ran through the plan in his mind. By the time he reached the Fontaine Saint-Sulpice, Reiniger knew one thing for sure – Blake and his friends weren't making it out of the building alive.

TWENTY

The automatic lights kicked out a flood of luminescence as Leopold stepped into the deserted hallway. The office building had been easy enough to breach thanks to a poorly-secured skylight, and most of the interior doors were unlocked. In the harsh neon light, Leopold could understand why – most of the offices were stripped bare, leaving empty expanses of dusty carpet and rows of deserted cubicles.

"What is this place?" whispered Sophie, as they made their way through the corridor.

"Looks like whoever was here moved on a long time ago. Did you send Mary our rendezvous point?"

"*Oui*, but what if the police pick up my SMS?"

"When they check for cell phone usage, it'll take them some time to sift through the background noise. By which time, we'll be long gone."

"Gone where?"

He ignored her question. Turning a corner, Leopold noticed a stairwell door at the end of the hallway and waved Sophie forward.

"The parking basement is this way." He led Sophie down the bare concrete steps at speed, their footsteps echoing against the cold walls as they descended into the belly of the abandoned office block. Leopold could taste the dust and damp, the unmistakable scent of neglect hanging heavy in the air.

"How will she get in?" Sophie asked, as they reached the bottom and made for the door. "This place is locked up."

"She's a cop, so I doubt she'll have much of a problem breaking into an empty building. Just hope the police don't get the same idea." He rattled the handle. "Locked. Dammit."

"You've not had much luck with doors today." She stepped forward.

He caught the faint scent of her perfume as she passed and felt his spirits lift momentarily. He shook it off.

"Looks like we're going to have to find another way out," she said, leaning hard against the door. "This thing won't move."

"Looks like lady luck's decided to leave us both hung out to dry."

"So melodramatic," said Sophie, rolling her eyes. "Maybe we can –" A sudden noise cut her off.

Glancing down, Leopold saw the door handle shake violently. He took a step back. "Get behind me and keep quiet."

"Hey!" she protested as Leopold yanked her backward.

"Shh. Try to resist the urge to open your mouth for once."

Fuming, Sophie bit her lip and complied. The door handle shook again, faster this time, and Leopold heard a loud *thump* from the other side of the wall. He tensed, ready to move.

"What do we do?" she hissed.

Leopold raised his finger to his lips, keeping his eyes fixed on the doorway. He caught the faint but unmistakable sound of metal on metal, then a series of clicks. The sound of lock tumblers falling into place.

"Get ready." He put his hand on Sophie's shoulder.

"For what?"

The door flew open. Leopold saw a sinewy figure stride toward them, obscured by the shadows. His fists clenched tight, he waited for the right moment. He could make out the figure's face in the dull light. A face he recognized.

"Mary?" He stepped forward. "What the hell took you so long?"

Mary whipped around. "Dammit, don't do that," she snapped. "It's bad enough I've got to find my way around this creepy place in the dark. I don't need people jumping out of the shadows at me."

Leopold raised his palms. "Okay, okay. Can you get us out of here?"

"There's an old access hatch that leads up to street level, just across the other side of the parking lot. The lock was practically rusted off. We should be able to get out onto the main road without being spotted. Assuming the police haven't decided to broaden their search perimeter, that is."

"As far as they know we're still running around inside the station. But they'll figure it out eventually."

"We'd better get going then." She paused, glancing down at Sophie. "Who's this?"

"Mary Jordan, meet Sophie Bardot," said Leopold, helping the art restorer to her feet. "I'm sure you'll get along just fine."

"Save the pleasantries for later," said Mary, looking Sophie up and down. "Follow me."

Setting at a brisk pace, the NYPD sergeant led the way through into the gloomy parking lot. "Are you going to tell me what the hell is going on?" she asked, not breaking her stride. "And what happened to Jerome?"

"It's a long story," said Leopold.

"Then tell it quickly."

"I was hired to consult for the Louvre. While I was there, I discovered a major security flaw and informed the art director. Jerome and I left to speak with *Mademoiselle* Bardot, which is when I got the call."

"What call?"

"The art director was murdered shortly after we left the museum. The police got hold of my cell phone number and asked me down to the station."

"Jesus, Leopold, what are you getting me into? And why the hell did you bring her along?"

"She insisted."

Mary shook her head. "You're kidding me. Where do you find these people?"

"We were taken into an interview room," Leopold continued, ignoring her. "They told us a fingerprint had been found near the murder scene. My fingerprint. You can figure out the rest."

"So this is a frame job?"

"Looks like it."

"But why?"

"That's what we need to figure out," said Leopold. "I'll need you to pull some favors. Think you can do that without raising any red flags?"

"If I act fast, sure."

He nudged Mary as they walked. "Just like old times."

"Don't get cute."

"*Excusez-moi*," said Sophie. "Can we do this later? I want answers too, don't forget that."

"Just let me handle this," said Mary. "Keep close behind and try to stay quiet."

"Let's just try to keep this civil, shall we?" said Leopold.

"Don't talk to me about civil; I'm not the one bossing everyone around," said Sophie. "Why should I have to listen to her?"

"Shh." Mary hissed, stopping in her tracks. "Keep still and don't make a sound."

"Why?"

Mary's gaze locked onto something. Something Leopold couldn't make out.

"There's someone else here."

TWENTY-ONE

Reiniger tightened his grip on his firearm, his index finger brushing the trigger. In the cool darkness of the subterranean parking lot, the assassin watched his quarry approach. It had been too easy to follow the lady cop. She hadn't even been paying attention. But now something seemed to have caught her eye.

Holding his position, Reiniger reminded himself that the human eye was nowhere near sensitive enough to pick out his shape in the shadows. Still twenty feet away, Reiniger calculated his targets' angle of escape was too wide for him to cover properly with the handgun. The chances of one or more of them diving for cover was too high, and Reiniger didn't relish the thought of chasing anyone around in the dark.

He shifted his gaze toward Blake and saw him take a step backward. The cop didn't move a muscle. The assassin felt his pulse quicken, felt the adrenaline kick in.

Time to move.

He surged forward, gun raised. "This is not the time to consider running." His voice was calm and authoritative. "This can be over quickly and painlessly. Or, I can take my time with you. The choice is yours."

No reply.

"Please, step out from behind Mr. Blake." The assassin waved a gloved hand, beckoning the younger woman forward.

"Sophie, stay where you are," the cop said. "He needs us to spread out so he can kill us quicker. He knows he doesn't have time to take any chances."

The bitch was right. Reiniger decided to kill her first. He pointed the gun at the cop's forehead and squeezed the trigger. He felt the hammer cock.

"*Ne bougez pas!*" A voice from behind. A flurry of heavy footsteps.

The assassin whipped around and dropped to his knees, targeting the three armed police officers advancing across the empty lot. He brought the pistol up and fired a double tap, aiming for center mass. The rounds hit home, knocking the nearest target on his back, unconscious.

With a split second of purchased time, Reiniger considered his options. The response team would call for backup soon, if they hadn't already, and more armed police were only seconds away. With more guns and body armor. The assassin knew he had only two choices – either kill Blake and the others and almost certainly be gunned down himself, or retreat. The latter option seemed preferable.

Instinct taking over, Reiniger dove behind a concrete pillar as the sound of gunfire erupted behind him. Peering into the gloom, Reiniger scanned the area for movement. A muzzle flash sent him ducking back for cover a split second before the bullet tore into the space where his head had been. The impact sent up a tiny plume of dust. A second and third shot kept him pinned. He knew the tactic well – the shooter's partner would be moving in for the kill, relying on his teammate to provide a distraction.

Big mistake.

Reiniger ducked to the side as another staccato flash lit up the parking lot. He closed his eyes and concentrated, listening for any sign of approach. Another shot, and the sound of bullets ricocheting off the walls. In between flashes the sound of heavy soles falling lightly on the ground.

Another shot. Another flash.

Reiniger heard the scuffle again and tensed, his target no more than a couple of feet away. With the pistol still in his hand, the assassin stepped out from behind the pillar and attacked. Before the cop could react, Reiniger thrust the butt of his gun into the man's throat and felt something crunch.

Another shot came from behind and the cop's knees buckled. Reiniger angled his gun and squeezed the trigger, sending a round straight through the man's skull. The bullet passed through the cop's helmet and out the other side, lost in the darkness. The officer crumpled to the floor and Reiniger pressed his back against the column, out of sight.

As the next gunshot came and went, the assassin ducked out from behind the pillar. The gray outline of the remaining police officer was unmistakable, even in the low light. Reiniger fired two rapid shots to the man's chest. He went down hard. Reiniger scanned the parking lot for any sign of backup before turning to the spot where Blake and the others had stood moments earlier.

They were gone.

TWENTY-TWO

"Keep moving!"

Leopold felt Mary's hand on his back, pushing him forward. He grunted from the pain radiating from his shoulder and stumbled, his vision beginning to blur. The harsh neons that lit up the deserted corridors made him feel nauseous, so he took a moment to lean up against the wall and catch his breath.

"What's wrong? We need to get out of here," said Mary, tugging at his sleeve. "Whoever's still alive down there is going to be coming for us."

"Just give me a minute," he said, clutching his shoulder.

"What happened?" Mary took his hand and pulled it away. "Jesus!"

Blake stared down at his hand. It was slick with blood.

"He's been shot. We have to get him to a hospital," said Sophie.

"That's not going to happen," said Mary. "If we show up with a bullet wound, they'll call the police. We need to get somewhere safe. I can stitch him up if the injury is clean enough." She pulled Leopold forward. "It just looks like a graze. Nothing a few stitches can't fix. All things considered, you're pretty lucky."

"Great, that makes me feel much better."

"Don't be such a baby. Can you walk?"

He nodded.

"Good. You got any idea in that big brain of yours where we might be able to hide out while we get this mess sorted out?"

Leopold blinked hard and felt his vision start to clear. "Give me your cell phone."

Mary passed the handset over. "This isn't the time to be making calls."

"Just give me a minute." He accessed the unit's internet browser and punched in a web address. "My company owns property in Paris, but I need to check where." He logged into the Blake Investments secure server and loaded up the files he needed. "We've got a shareholding in a small tenement building along the Champs-Élysées. Looks like we've rented most of the apartments out to the office workers, but there look to be a few that are unoccupied." He looked up. "You know, layoffs."

"Can you find out which ones are empty?"

"Not from this." He paused. "But I've got a contact in one of the legal departments we can use. He heads up the commercial property division."

"And he can get this information for us now?"

"Should be fine. He's been begging for a raise for months." Leopold smiled and handed back the phone. "I've just sent him an email. We should hear back soon. In the meantime, we can head in that direction."

Sophie leaned in, a look of concern in her eyes. "Can you make it that far in your condition?"

He caught the scent of her perfume again, intensified by her elevated body temperature. The smell jostled something in his nerves, making his skin tingle. His shoulder throbbed in protest and Leopold snapped out of his daze. "I don't have much of a choice, do I? The police will be preoccupied with whoever the hell it was that just killed those cops, so that gives us a small window of opportunity. Is there another way out of here?"

"The alleyway behind the building is fenced off from the main road," said Mary. "I doubt anyone's going to be searching there for a while."

"How do we get there?" asked Sophie.

"There's only one way down. We're going to have to open a window and jump."

"You've got to be kidding," said Leopold. "In case you hadn't noticed, I've been shot. I'm hardly in any condition to be jumping from anywhere."

"Man up a little. Just tuck and roll when you hit the floor and try to land on your good shoulder. It's either that or we get the prison doctor to stitch you up."

"Have I ever told you how much I miss these conversations?"

Mary shot him a look.

"Fine, okay, so we're jumping for it. Any idea which direction we need to go?"

"The west side of the building faces out to the alleyway," she replied, examining her cell phone's compass application. "Which is in this direction." She stalked off toward one of the empty offices at the other end of the corridor. "Try to keep up."

Leopold looked up at Sophie, who held out her hand.

"Better do as she says, *non?*"

He nodded. "Just try not to use me to break your fall. I'm feeling a little fragile."

She smiled and helped him back onto his feet and they set off in pursuit of Mary, who had disappeared into the empty office beyond. They rounded the corner and Leopold spotted her wrestling with one of the floor-to-ceiling windows that overlooked the street outside.

"Here, give me a hand with this."

Between the three of them, they managed to wrench the large panel open, letting in the cool night air and the rumbling sounds of the city. Leopold looked down.

"We're a good twenty feet up," he said, turning to Sophie. "If we land properly, there shouldn't be any problem."

"And how do we do that?"

"Keep your feet and knees together to avoid twisting an ankle. Bend your legs but keep them firmly stiff. As soon as your feet touch the ground, collapse into a roll on one side. That will absorb most of the impact force and stop you from shattering your ankles."

Sophie nodded, clearly not convinced.

"Don't worry, you'll be just fine," he said, putting his hand on her shoulder and leaving a rusty smudge of blood on her jacket. "Sorry." He pulled his hand away.

"So, are we heading for the car?"

"That's not an option," said Mary. "The police have the roads blocked off. Thankfully, there's quite a crowd forming outside, so if we can get through to the other side of the alleyway, there's a chance we can slip through unnoticed while they're preoccupied. If we don't get stopped, we can make our way on foot from there until we can flag down a taxi. How far is the apartment?"

"About three miles north of here," said Leopold. "Assuming I don't pass out on the way, we should be able to make it."

"Is he always like this?" asked Sophie.

Mary sighed and nodded. "Comes with the territory, I'm afraid." She turned to Leopold. "Time to get moving. After you." She gestured toward the open window.

"I guess I had that coming." He clutched his injured shoulder. Stepping forward, Leopold looked out of the window to the dark alley floor. Taking a deep breath, he clambered out into the night, one leg either side of the frame, and got ready for the jump. Despite the fears and uncertainties that played on his mind, he had no doubts about one thing – this was going to hurt like hell.

TWENTY-THREE

The environmental controls onboard The *Thanatos* were designed to simulate the passing of night and day. With most of the crew below deck and without access to natural light, the systems helped keep everyone's circadian rhythm synchronized.

James Cullen's quarters were housed near the center of the ship, where the movements of the waves were less disruptive. The senior operative lay on his bed, reading a book on his tablet computer. Inside the room, the temperature and lighting controls were set to night-time and the ship's clock reminded him it was too late to still be awake. As he leaned over to turn out the lights, a gentle knock at the door made him look up.

"Come in."

The door slid open and Rose stepped through, dressed in tight jeans and a fitted tee. She was carrying a laptop under one arm.

"It's a little late for social calls," said James, sitting up.

"Sorry, boss. I had something I needed to show you."

He patted the mattress and she took a seat next to him. Even in the low light, she looked stunning – the snug fabric of her clothes accentuating all the right places.

"What is it?" he asked, catching the scent of her perfume.

"You got anything to drink?"

He nodded toward the chest of drawers against the far wall. "There's a bottle of Mount Gay in there and some glasses."

Rose set the laptop on the bed and fetched the rum. She poured two measures of the amber liquor and handed one to James. They both took a sip.

"Cheers," she said, and they clinked glasses.

"So what did you have to show me that requires a toast?"

"I wouldn't say we needed to toast anything, I was just desperate for a drink." She smiled. "Although I do have some more dirt on this Blake guy. Wanna see?"

James raised his glass in the affirmative.

"Here, take a look at this." She opened the laptop and the system sprang into life. "According to the records I pulled from the European Business Register, Blake's company has been buying up dying corporations throughout the EU, especially in the west. They strip the businesses down to the bone, selling off everything until the company is essentially just a name on a piece of paper."

James leaned forward. "This guy just gets more and more interesting, doesn't he?"

"After that, the trail went cold. So I asked one of the guys in the programming lab to follow the money trail and look where it led." She pointed to something on the screen.

"What the hell is that?"

113

"Something Blake Industries wanted to keep off the books. Some kind of research facility, apparently set up under the guise of a non-profit."

"They went to a lot of trouble to hide this."

"Understatement of the year. With over a dozen parent companies and umbrella corporations, you'd need to know exactly where to look to even find a mention of these guys."

"And Blake kept his name out of it?"

"Yeah, look at this." She scrolled through the document. "A few years ago he resigned as director and appointed a trustee to run everything for him. He even gave up all the voting rights his shares carried. For all intents and purposes, he has absolutely zero legal liability for this place."

"Meaning what?"

"Meaning if anyone starts sniffing around, he has plausible deniability."

"I'm starting to see what the Director sees in this guy." He finished his drink, feeling the warmth spread through his chest. "What did you tell your friend?"

"Huh?"

"The programming guy."

"I just said I was following a lead for something."

"You trust him?"

Rose drained her own glass. "Yeah, of course. Don't worry," she put down her drink and moved toward him. "I've got us covered."

James felt his heart thump against his chest as Rose came closer. The scent of her perfume intensified. "You'd better," he said, smiling.

"You giving me my orders now, boss?" She rested one hand on his thigh.

"Don't tempt me."

"Just as well, you'd have your work cut out."

"You sure about that?"

She repositioned herself on the bed, resting on her hands and knees. James felt her hand move up his leg.

"How about we find out?" she said.

"You've had too much to drink."

"Stop trying to be chivalrous and come here." She grabbed hold of his t-shirt and pulled him forward.

Obliging, James leaned into her, one hand against the small of her back. As his lips met hers, he felt her spine arch and the hairs on his arms stood on end. She tasted like rum: dark and sweet, intoxicating. Her breathing was heavy, forcing her chest up and down in rhythm with her heartbeat. He pulled off his t-shirt and forced her in closer, feeling the warmth of her body against his skin.

Rose broke away for a brief moment and turned off the light. "I've been wanting to do that for six months."

"Me too, I think —"

"Don't talk," she said, climbing back on top of him. "We've got a lot of catching up to do."

TWENTY-FOUR

The somber outline of the Arc de Triomphe rose into the glassy night sky as Leopold, Mary, and Sophie clambered out of the taxi and stepped out onto the Champs-Élysées; Paris' answer to New York's Fifth Avenue. Despite the late hour, the streets were packed with diners and partygoers, and the manicured trees that lined the sidewalks were lit up with golden lights that bathed the entire neighborhood in a warm glow. The effect was one that Leopold associated with sitting too close to a Christmas tree.

"Where to now?" asked Mary, handing a fistful of change to the driver.

"My contact Harris arranged for the concierge to leave a set of keys for us. Thankfully, we pay them enough that they don't feel the need to ask questions. It's this way. Follow me." He strode out toward the other side of the road, weaving in and out of the slow moving traffic. Once safely across, he led the way toward an ornate apartment building, set back from the road and positioned above an expensive-looking restaurant.

"Wait a minute," Mary called out. "We're supposed to just waltz in there looking like this?" She pointed at

Leopold's shoulder, where a crimson blood stain had started to spread through his clothes.

"Normally, I'd agree," he said. "But don't worry, Harris has arranged everything." He set off again at a brisk pace. "It's quicker just to show you."

He took them past the main entrance, ignoring the immaculately dressed doorman, and ducked around the corner where the crowds were noticeably thinner and the lighting a little more subdued. Pulling out Sophie's cell phone, he checked the email message one more time.

"This way." He ducked through a gate and stepped into a deserted courtyard. Half a dozen industrial-sized dumpsters lined the walls and there was a distinct smell of rotting food and grease in the air. A dim halogen light cast a gloomy haze over the scene.

"Not exactly what I expected," said Mary. "But I guess everyone's trash smells the same."

Leopold walked toward a rusted metal door at the other end of the courtyard and reached for the handle. "If everything's gone as planned this should be unlocked." He pulled the handle and felt the latch click open with a satisfying *clunk*.

"Finally," said Sophie. "It's about time you figured out how to use doors."

"Shh. Keep quiet and follow me. We're going in through the back." He stepped into the corridor. The hallway was empty, silent except for the distant sound of a busy Parisian kitchen.

He pressed on. From ahead came a rising cacophony of metallic noise, steel against steel, and loud voices. A heady aroma filled his nose, a mixture of garlic and herbs. Late service was in full swing. "We're close," he said, turning to face the others. "All we have to do is get through the kitchens to the service elevator, and then ride up to the sixth floor. The keys have been hidden outside the apartment, ready for us to collect."

"And we're suppose to sneak through a kitchen full of chefs without being spotted?" asked Mary.

"These guys will be so busy concentrating on their work, they won't notice us. If anyone asks, we're the health inspectors."

They reached the end of the hallway and were greeted by a set of double doors, designed to swing open and allow the serving staff easy passage. He felt a blast of warm air hit his face as he pushed through, taking a second to get his bearings in the chaos that greeted him.

The kitchens were a galley design, relatively narrow but long enough that the dozen chefs each had plenty of space to go about their work. The aromas from the myriad of dishes was overwhelming, and Leopold suddenly remembered he hadn't eaten anything since breakfast. Setting a brisk pace, he headed toward the far end of the kitchen and kept his head down, not making eye contact. He held his arms at his side, trying not to knock anything over.

A blast of yellow flame erupted a few feet from his face as he skirted one of the gas stoves. He saw one of the chefs pour a slosh of liquor into a smoking-hot saucepan, resulting in more fire. A little further down, another cook was slicing open a roasted pigeon breast, revealing a moist, pink center that made Leopold's stomach growl. Ahead, a gaggle of young commis chefs were busy preparing raw vegetables and salads, tossing the skins into a trash can near the exit door. None of them noticed Leopold, Mary, and Sophie brush past and made their way for the door.

"This way." Leopold held the door open. "The service elevator should be around here somewhere."

"Over there." Sophie pointed to a rusty metal grate as they rounded the corner. "It doesn't look very safe."

Leopold grabbed hold of the iron rails and heaved the gate open. Once they were all inside, he selected the sixth floor. The elevator shuddered to life and began its ascent, jostling and rumbling all the way up, much to Sophie's intense discomfort.

"Relax," said Leopold. "We're nearly there. I don't know about you, but some dinner and a few hours' sleep would do me a world of good."

She tensed as the elevator rattled to an abrupt stop.

"Here we go." He pulled back the railings and stepped out into the hallway.

He led the others through the service entrance and into the main corridor, along the plush carpets toward apartment 601. As the email message had promised, a neatly trimmed Ficus near the front door concealed the keycard that would let them in. Sliding the card across a magnetic strip mounted into the wall, Leopold heard the door click open. He stepped over the threshold, activating the automatic lights.

Although considerably smaller than his own New York City apartment, Leopold still couldn't help but be impressed by the penthouse's tasteful décor and clever use of space. The softly lit reception hall was large enough for a small group to stand at arms' length. It led through to a cavernous drawing room to one side and a kitchen and dining room to the other. On the other side of the apartment, a corridor led away out of sight, presumably to the bedrooms and bathrooms.

Mary clucked her tongue as she entered. "Nice to see how the other half lives. Makes me appreciate the simple things in life."

"I think my whole apartment could fit inside this room," said Sophie. "And you said that nobody lives here?"

"It's on long-term lease," replied Leopold. "The previous tenant moved back to the States and hasn't been able to sublet it yet. So don't worry about anyone walking in on us."

"I wasn't worried about that," said Sophie, pointing at something behind him. "I was more concerned about the man standing in the living room holding the gun."

TWENTY-FIVE

Leopold whipped around. Ahead, a tall silhouette strode confidently toward them, a gun held by his side. The consultant tensed, ready to fight. The figure spoke.

"*Monsieur* Blake, I was sent here by your contact, *Monsieur* Harris. He was concerned for your safety. Were you followed?"

The tall man's voice was deep and thickly accented, but the tone seemed sincere. Leopold watched him holster the handgun. "And you are?" he asked, noticing the man's features as his eyes adjusted to the light. He wore a finely tailored suit, a Gaultier.

"My name is Gerard. I understand from M. Harris that your usual bodyguard, Jerome, is otherwise engaged. I am here to act as his replacement while you are in need of me."

"I don't think that will be necessary."

"M. Harris and I disagree, I'm afraid, sir. I will stay close by while you rest and eat, and then we will have to move on."

"Move on?" asked Sophie. "This place looks safe to me."

Leopold turned to look at her. "This place is connected to me through my company, which means we'll be found eventually. The police will be a while, but whoever tried to take us out in the parking lot – he's got me worried."

"I wasn't briefed on this," said Gerard. "There is someone else tracking you?"

"Tell me what you know so far," said Leopold. "What did Harris say?"

"Only what you sent in your first email: that you had run into some issues with local law enforcement and required extraction as soon as possible. M. Harris contacted me to arrange your passage here and to stay on hand until you could get out of the country."

"I'm afraid leaving Paris isn't an option until we figure out who's trying to take me out. Otherwise I'll never stop running."

"What do you propose we do?"

"Simple. We look at the evidence and figure out why someone would want me locked up. Once we understand the motive, we can figure out who's most likely to gain from this mess and the rest will fall into place."

"When did you last eat?"

"This morning. Why?"

"Your brain, as well as your body, will work better when it's not craving food. You need calories to function. Fortunately, we are in France." Gerard strode through into the kitchen. "*Allez*, come on through. I brought enough food to get you all back on your feet."

Mary raised an eyebrow. "Jerome never cooks," she whispered. "I think you're on to a good thing here, Leopold."

They followed the bodyguard through, settled themselves around the dining table, and waited for Gerard to prepare their meal.

"You'll need to stitch up that shoulder," said Gerard, fishing a small box out of a cupboard. "Use this. I assume you know what you're doing?" He tossed the box to Mary.

She caught the med kit in one hand. "Shouldn't be a problem, just so long as he doesn't start squirming around." She fished out a long needle, some antiseptic and gauze. As she threaded the needle, her cell phone rang.

"Who's calling?" asked Leopold.

"The cop back in New York just emailed some files over on the Notre Dame murder victims. I also asked him to run a license plate for me. Now, roll up your sleeve and let's get started."

Leopold turned his shoulder. As Mary leaned in close, he noticed the damage for the first time. The bullet had torn a deep gash in the fleshy part of his shoulder. Wincing, he tried not to move as she applied the antiseptic and began to stitch him up.

In the kitchen, Gerard busied himself preparing dinner. He pulled down a selection of saucepans and opened the refrigerator. He fired up the burners and doused the pans in a liberal helping of olive oil and butter. Leopold felt his mouth begin to water as the smells drifted over to the dining table.

"I'll be done soon," said Mary. "Just hold still."

Within a few minutes, the final stitch had been sewn and Gerard was laying out steaming bowls of delicious-smelling food. The meal was exquisite, a brothy mix of

French sausage with glistening butter beans and generous hunks of bacon, leeks, and fresh herbs.

"Here, drink this." Gerard handed each of them a bottle of dark beer.

The warmth of the food immediately improving his mood, Leopold took a swig from the beer and felt the throbbing in his shoulder subdue slightly.

"Wow, this is good," said Mary. "We'll have to keep you around, Gerard. Aren't you having any?"

"There's meat and eggs for me, but I'm not due a meal for forty-five minutes," he said, stacking the dirty pans into the dishwasher. "Once you've eaten, we'll discuss the plan. I would recommend finding a safe house in the morning, based on what you've told me."

"Tell me about these files," said Leopold, finishing a mouthful. "Who were the victims?"

Mary consulted her cell phone. "We know about Director Dubois already," she took a gulp of beer. "According to the email, the other four victims appear to have been chosen at random. The second target was Virginie Bernard, a forty-three-year-old homemaker from Paris. She was meeting a friend for lunch and never showed. Second up," she squinted at the screen, "is Jun Akanishi, a telecoms worker from Japan here on vacation with his family. Next is Gunther Bauer, a German contractor here on business. The final victim is Amélie Ledoyen, a senior associate at Phillippe Jacques, one of the big law firms."

"And they were killed by the person trying to set up Leopold?" asked Sophie, polishing off the last of her meal. "Why would the killer go to all that trouble to kill four random people afterwards?"

"Why are we assuming the others were picked at random?" said Leopold.

"You think there's a connection?"

"We can safely assume that killing the director was an easy way to link me to the murder, but what if the sniper had more than one target? The first, Dubois, was meant to ensure my capture and incarceration, and the second... well, that's the question. What else do we have on these people?"

"I've got full bios attached to the email." Mary turned to Gerard. "You got a printer around here somewhere?"

The bodyguard handed her a slip of paper. "Here's the wi-fi codes. I checked the network for bugs already. Once you're in, you can send the files to the printer wirelessly."

She tapped a few keys on her phone. "Done. Where can I pick them up?"

"The study is down the corridor at the far side of the apartment. Follow me," He led them through the living room and down the hallway. "Help yourselves." He opened one of the doors and waved them through.

The study was impressive, featuring an array of razor-thin computer monitors, wall-to-wall bookcases, and a plush seating area opposite the desk. The room smelled like furniture polish and leather.

Leopold spotted the printer and pulled out the stack of paper from the tray. "Let's take a look, shall we?"

"I'll be watching the front door," said Gerard. "There's an intercom on the wall if you need me." He slipped out.

"Wow, this place is *incroyable*," said Sophie. "Look at all these books." She ran her finger along their spines.

"Homer, Virgil, Dostoyevsky, Francis Bacon. Quite a collection."

"Any James Patterson?" asked Mary.

"It doesn't look like it. Although, who knows – maybe he has an ebook collection hidden away on a Kindle somewhere."

"Can we get back on topic?" said Leopold. "We need to find a connection between these victims. Here," he spread the paper out on the coffee table. "You two read through these, and I'll get onto the computer. I should be able to get us some outside help."

He waited for them to take a seat and went over to the desk, settling himself into the chair. He tapped the space bar and the trio of LED monitors jumped into life. Accessing the operating system, Leopold fired up the internet browser. "Anything yet?" he asked.

"There's quite a lot here," Mary replied. "It'll take some time. What are you looking for?"

Leopold punched in a postal code. "You and I both know a little something about police procedure. Rousseau isn't going to stop hunting me down until I've found enough evidence to clear my name. Or until I'm dead. I'd rather avoid the latter option."

"We need to figure out why Dubois was targeted. I mean, he must have been killed for a reason, right?"

"Right."

"Did you find anything while you were at the Louvre?"

Leopold nodded. "One of the Da Vinci paintings, 'The Virgin and Child with Saint Anne', had been replaced with a fake. Jerome and I were in the middle of tracking down some leads when all this mess started."

126

Mary looked over at Sophie. "And I'm guessing this young lady was first on your list."

"I had nothing to do with any paintings being stolen," said Sophie. "I had taken a few days off, that's all. Sick leave."

"You don't look all that sick to me."

"I've had other things to worry about."

Mary turned back to Leopold. "Well, whatever happened to that painting, if Dubois was involved that at least gives us something to go on. But without proof we're a little stuck."

The consultant smiled. "So let's go find some proof."

"Where?"

"If Dubois had anything to do with the theft, he'll have the original painting stored somewhere. Somewhere he'd be able to keep a very close eye on at all times."

Mary leaned forward in her chair. "Like a storage locker? Or a safety deposit box? There must be thousands of those in the city."

"This is far too valuable a prize, especially to an art lover like Dubois. No, he'd want to keep the painting close by, somewhere only he had access." He tilted one of the monitors toward the others and tapped the screen. "If I were him, I'd keep it at home, somewhere out of sight."

"That's Dubois' place? It's huge. Where would we even start looking?"

"Sophie, you knew the director well."

She nodded.

"Did you ever visit him at home?"

"*Oui*, of course. His wife used to teach me to cook when I was a girl." She bit her lip. "I'm sorry, it's… it's just difficult thinking that I'll never see him again."

"I know it's hard, but try to think back. Did you ever see anything in his house that might look like a place to hide something? Something he couldn't afford to lose."

She thought for a moment. "The house is quite large, but if I know Jean, he would want the painting to be kept somewhere special. Somewhere that would feel right to him."

"And do you know where that might be?"

"Jean kept a lot of artwork. It was quite a collection. He even had his own private gallery on the top floor. I guess if he had something to do with this missing painting, he would keep it there. But I still find it hard to believe he would do something… so terrible. He was a good man, *Monsieur* Blake. He had his faults, but he was still a good man."

"Even the best of us can make bad decisions," said Mary. "At least, from the sound of it he had nothing to do with the murders. And if we can track down this painting, maybe we'll get some answers."

"He would never hurt anyone," said Sophie, wiping her eyes with the back of her hand.

"But it looks like he got mixed up with a bunch of people who would," said Leopold. "Killing Dubois was just the start. Whoever's behind this wanted me and Jerome out of the picture, too. Along with anyone else who gets in the way."

"In the way of what?" asked Mary. "That's what we're missing here. All I do know is that prison isn't exactly the safest place to be, even when you're not being hunted down. It would be all too easy to arrange for one of the inmates to take you out and it would look like just a random act of violence."

"Except that I never made it to the prison," said Leopold. "And now whoever's behind all this is going to be working on a contingency plan."

"That would explain why that man attacked us in the parking lot," said Sophie. "He might have been following us the whole time."

"I did notice something earlier," said Mary, taking her seat once again. "On the drive from the airport, a car was following us. It might have been nothing, but I asked the precinct to run the plates. The results should be in here somewhere." She flipped through the stack of paper. "Look at this."

Sophie took the printout and read it aloud. "Black Volkswagen Passat, registered to Marius Schwartz of Berlin, Germany. No outstanding tickets or warrants." She looked up. "So what's the big deal?"

"Read the next part."

"Marius Schwartz, born in Frankfurt, Germany, in 1974..." she paused. "Died of a heart attack nearly a year ago. *Merde.*"

"So either Herr Schwartz is driving from beyond the grave, or someone didn't want to take any risks with his real identity," said Mary.

"I guess we're not going to get that vacation after all," said Leopold.

"We'd better get this information to Gerard."

"Get him in here, we don't have much time. We need to figure this out before Jerome winds up in the middle of a prison riot. Thanks to me, he's walking right into a trap."

TWENTY-SIX

Marty Jackson lay on the thin prison mattress and felt the steel springs dig into his spine. The guards had called lights out hours earlier, but something in the air was keeping him awake, something he couldn't quite put his finger on. Elsewhere in the block water was leaking onto the floor. In the silence, the drip, drip, drip of water on the hard tile was impossible to ignore, meaning another night of staring at the ceiling was in the cards. Again.

Letting out a deep sigh, Marty squeezed his eyes shut and tried to force his brain to stop whirring. He pictured open fields, blue skies, and anything else he could think of that might soothe him off to sleep. A crashing waterfall. Birdsong. The smell of money.

The sound of approaching footsteps was not on the list. Nor was the screech of his cell door sliding open. He sat up in the top bunk and watched as three men entered, two of them wearing guard's uniforms. The third guy was a good six inches taller than the others and built like a pro-wrestler. His skin was black enough that Marty struggled to make out his shape in the low light, but it was obvious the man was huge.

"*Ta gueule*. Lie back down," one of the guards ordered, his English a little rusty. "New prisoner transfer."

The officers unlocked a set of cuffs and the giant man rubbed his wrists. The two guards left the cell and the bars slid closed behind them. The big guy looked up.

Marty shuffled to the edge of his bed. "You speak English?"

No reply.

"C'mon, buddy. I don't speak a word of French, you're gonna have to meet me in the middle. What's your name?"

The stranger ignored the question and sat down on the lower bunk, making the bed frame creak.

"We're gonna be here a while," he continued. "You gotta talk to me eventually. I'm Marty Jackson, currently on year two of a five year stretch. What you in for?"

No reply.

"I was sent down for extortion. Alleged, of course. Whatever you did to get yourself here, I'm sure you're as innocent as me." He lay back down. "Anyways, I'll look forward to talking some more in the morning." Marty closed his eyes, letting his new roommate settle in for the night. The dripping noise had stopped and the cell block was silent.

Marty ignored his better judgment and sat up again. "Listen, buddy. It's gonna be bad enough for you in here without going out of your way to piss people off. Take it from me, man. Try to show a little respect. There's guys in gen pop that'll take great pleasure in making an example out of you."

Still no reply.

"Fine, you're on your own." He flopped back onto the bed and tried to get comfortable. He heard a rustling noise and opened his eyes again. The stranger was standing up, eyes level with the top bed.

"In the morning, show me these people," he said. "I'd like an introduction."

And then he was gone. The bed frame creaked and Marty screwed his eyes shut, his pulse thumping in his ears. Something about the stranger's voice sent chills down his spine. He tried to think happy thoughts. None came.

TWENTY-SEVEN

Reiniger dropped the stick shift into fourth gear and floored the gas pedal, feeling the turbocharger kick in and press him back into the driver's seat. Now away from the crowded roads in the center of the city, he felt more comfortable putting his foot down and putting as much distance between him and the *Commissariat Central* as possible. The two liter diesel under the hood growled as the turbo eased off, and Reiniger settled into a comfortable cruising speed as the road opened up ahead. A call came through the car's speakers and Reiniger activated the VW's built-in telephone. The incoming number was blocked.

"You're behind schedule." The voice on the other end of the line came through loud and clear. "Update me on your progress."

"I delivered Blake and his bodyguard into police custody, as requested."

"You're stalling. I have eyes on the situation. I know what happened. Can I trust you to rectify this?"

"Blake and a third individual, a young woman, escaped from the holding cell, presumably with help from the bodyguard. They rendezvoused with Sergeant

Jordan." He paused. "Their whereabouts are currently unknown."

There was a brief moment of silence.

"Tell me your location."

Reiniger shifted into sixth gear and eased off the gas a little. "The police interrupted. I'm en route to the office now."

"Negative. Blake has property in the city. I need you to head there."

"I'll need an address."

"Not over the phone. Check your inbox."

"Get me an I.D. on the younger woman."

"Done. I assume I don't need to remind you of the timescales we're working to."

"I still have fourteen hours," said Reiniger.

"Just make sure you get to them before the police do. Now he's seen you, I don't want him talking. Also be aware Blake's company employs a private security agency in the city. He'll have protection."

Reiniger hung up and accessed his email via the touchscreen panel built into the VW's console. The address had come through, a location several miles away near the Arc de Triomphe. Taking the next exit, the assassin found a secluded spot and parked. He used his cell phone to access a satellite map of the target area. Zooming in, he checked his internet browser any available information. He found several references to the ground floor restaurant, "La Gourmande", and a brief history of the building itself. Unfortunately, there were no floor plans. Still, more than enough to work with.

Stepping out into the cold night air, Reiniger popped the trunk and pulled out a suitcase full of fresh clothes.

He selected a charcoal Brioni suit and quickly changed, fastening the jacket over his gun and shoulder strap. Now more suitably dressed, he climbed back into the driver's seat and started the engine.

With the quickest route mapped out by the car's satellite navigation system, Reiniger set off along the Boulevard Périphérique back toward the heart of the city, grateful for the sparse traffic. He nudged the car a little above the speed limit and tried to focus. In less than thirty minutes, one way or another, this would all be over.

TWENTY-EIGHT

The air conditioning in the penthouse was set a little too cold and Mary was starting to feel the chill. While Leopold and Sophie busied themselves with the case files in the study, Mary had excused herself and gone looking for the master bedroom. Sure enough, whoever owned the place kept a Kindle on the nightstand. The e-reader was stuffed full of romance and erotica titles.

So much for classic literature, thought Mary, sitting down on the bed. The air in the bedroom was a little warmer, and the plush mattress was comfortable enough that Mary had to force herself not to lie down on it for fear of falling asleep. Instead, she took out her cell phone and stared at the screen. Another three missed calls.

She sighed, hit the redial button and heard the call connect.

"Mary, is that you?" her sister's voice came through the speaker.

"Yeah, it's me. Sorry I've not had chance to call you."

"Or pick up."

"I've been busy. Listen, Kate, mom told me you needed to talk. What do you want?"

There was a pause. "I know it's been a while."

"Five years. Not that anyone's counting."

"This isn't about you and me, Mary. This is more important than all that. I need to make sure you're going to be okay."

"Make sure I'm okay? Since when did you live up to that particular part of being a big sister?"

"What happened wasn't..." another pause. "Look, let's not get into this, okay? At least, not over the phone."

"Mom said you needed to get in touch urgently. If you aren't trying to mend bridges, what the hell do you want?"

"I'm worried about your safety."

"I'm a cop. I'm never going to be a hundred percent safe."

"That's not what I mean. I'm talking about the company you've been keeping recently. I'm talking about Blake. He's going to get you hurt, or worse."

"Who I choose to spend time with is none of your business," said Mary. "And I can take care of myself. I'm a big girl."

"This isn't just about my personal feelings toward the guy. Not that it's any secret I think he's an entitled, arrogant, selfish son of a bitch. But this isn't about that. He's going to wind up getting you killed."

"It's part of the job. Putting myself in harm's way is the price I have to pay for what I do. I don't take any unnecessary risks, not that I have to explain myself to you. When was the last time you put yourself in the line of fire?"

"You have no idea what I do," said Kate.

"You work for the World Health Organization. How dangerous could it be?"

"I see my fair share of action. But I'm not calling to argue with you, I'm trying to tell you something. Something important."

"Then spit it out." Mary got up from the bed and paced the room. "I need to get back to work."

Kate sighed. "As you know, Blake's company has its fingers in a lot of pies."

"Yeah, but nothing that worries me."

"Well, aside from the hedge funds, the military contracts, the energy divisions, he's also got an entire corporation set up for biological research. Medicines, vaccines, that sort of thing. It's called Chemworks."

"Doesn't sound particularly dangerous to me," said Mary.

"They stopped sharing their research with the public over three years ago. Since then, they've been focusing on something else."

"Like what?"

"Around the same time they closed their doors to the public, they started experimenting with particularly nasty strains of deadly viruses – modified H7N9, NCoV, Ebola, to name a few."

"Don't be ridiculous. You think Blake would let that happen?"

"That's the problem. The whole point of the research was to help people, but, like any scientific study, there are always unexpected side effects. We suspect they've stumbled across something that could be even worse than the diseases they were studying in the first place."

Mary clenched her teeth. "And you're coming to me with nothing more than the word of some informant? What is it you want me to do, exactly?"

"My informant has worked there since the beginning. He's seen how things have changed, but it's all been so gradual... before anyone knew what was happening, the management were shutting them off from the outside world – increasing security, making unexplained layoffs. I'm telling you, something bad is going on. And Blake is a part of it. Walk away. Just get on a plane and come back home."

"I don't need you or anyone else telling me what is and what isn't safe. I can make that call myself."

"No, you can't," said Kate. "Your objectivity is all screwed up. Think like a cop – either Blake knows about this and he's going along with it, or he doesn't know and there are people in his organization who are working against him. I don't even know which is worse. Either way, if this research gets into the wrong hands, it could be very dangerous. And not just for you, for all of us. Do you really want to be in the picture when this all comes out? People have been killed for far less."

"Like I said, I'm a big girl."

"Look, I just –"

Mary hung up and threw the cell phone across the room. It hit the armchair in the corner and bounced off onto the carpet. She took a moment to compose herself and decided to join the others, picking up her phone on the way out.

"How's it going?" she asked, walking into the study. "Any leads?"

"Nothing yet," said Leopold. "It looks like the victims were unconnected. I can't see any motive here."

"Are any of them connected with you or your company?" asked Mary. "Maybe that's the link."

"Not that I can tell from this information, though I can have someone back at the office check for sure. We use dozens of law firms and building contractors and many of our employees have spouses that stay at home. We've got offices in Japan, too. I can check, but I can't see how any of them could have done something to get them killed."

"What about the lawyer?"

Leopold shuffled through the stack of paper. "She worked for one of the big Paris firms."

"One of the firms your company used in the past?"

"Probably, yes. Though I can hardly keep track of everything that's going on."

Mary bit her lip. "But you make sure you've got people looking out for anything that might get you into trouble, right?"

"Sure, I have people I trust looking out for the good of the company. And looking out for me personally. Why?"

"Just wondering whether there might be some connection you're overlooking, that's all. Send the files through to your contact." She handed over her cell phone and turned to leave.

"Where are you going?"

Mary paused in the doorway. "I'm in desperate need of a hot shower."

TWENTY-NINE

Anton Rousseau sat in the cramped security office and scratched his three-day stubble. The tiny video monitor only produced a black and white image and the security cameras feeding it were old. The picture was blurry as hell. He played back the video again, tracking Blake and the others from their holding cell through to the roof and into the parking garage next door. The bodyguard was gone, but there was a fourth man now. Not part of the group. Rousseau watched the gunfight again. He watched Blake and the two women jump out a window. There weren't any cameras outside. He rewound the video and watched it again from the beginning.

Why do they always try to run? Rousseau rubbed his eyes with his knuckles. The telephone rang and he picked up.

"*Capitaine?*"

"*Oui*, speaking. What is it?"

"This is Antoine over in surveillance. We picked up some footage of three people matching the descriptions you sent. A hotel near the *Commissariat* sent a file over. You'll be glad to know it's in better condition than our own tapes."

"Anything useful on the video?"

"We've got them flagging down a cab a couple of blocks away. I'm in touch with the taxi company now, we should get a destination from them soon."

"*Bon*, let me know when you do." Rousseau hung up.

He turned back to the black and white screen and tapped the glass with a finger. To Rousseau, the world looked better in monochrome. There was less opportunity for confusion. The fourth man came on the screen again, holding the gun. Whoever he was, he fought well, putting two of Rousseau's men in the hospital and the other... The *Capitaine* frowned and balled up a fist. Whatever Blake was mixed up in, he wasn't going to last long without finding help from somewhere.

Rousseau figured the American would regroup and then attempt to flee. That's what most of them tried to do. Fortunately, it was a strategy that rarely worked. Instead, the fugitive always brought about their own destruction by venturing out into the open, falling for the allure of the 'make or break' escape. A better strategy would be to lay low and keep out of sight for six months. But nobody ever did.

Turning away from the monitors, Rousseau fired up the wheezing computer that took up most of the desk and accessed the web browser. He punched in a web address and accessed the Blake Investments company homepage, looking for regional offices in Paris. He found the La Defense branch after a few minutes. Rousseau printed out the details and picked up the phone, dialing an internal number.

"*Oui?*" a disinterested voice came on the line.

"This is *Capitaine* Rousseau. I need you to run a property search for any residential properties connected with Blake Investments or its subsidiaries. Focus on properties in Paris."

"*Pas de problème*, shouldn't take too long. When do you need it."

"Now. Call my mobile phone when it's done. I'll be on the road."

The captain hung up and got to his feet, slinging his jacket over his shoulder, and headed for the door. His car was parked nearby and Rousseau wanted to be in it when the call came through. He did his best thinking while driving, especially at night when the roads were empty and he could roll down the windows without being blasted with exhaust fumes.

Rousseau climbed into his unmarked car, a dark blue Renault, and coaxed it out of the parking lot and onto the road. He headed north and cleared his mind while he waited for the information. He didn't have to wait long.

"The taxi had several fares tonight, but only one that picked up anywhere near the *Commissariat Central*. The final drop point was on the Champs-Elysées," said the officer, his voice patched through to the car's wireless speakers.

"Any luck searching for properties nearby?"

"*Oui*, there's an apartment block there. All of the properties have been leased, so are probably occupied. Perhaps he went somewhere else."

"They might be leased, but that doesn't mean there's anyone living there right now. Call the concierge and find out."

"*Oui, Capitaine.*"

The line went dead and Rousseau turned the Renault around, heading in the direction of the Arc de

Triomphe. With the window down, a cool wind whipped at his hair and face, drowning out the noise of the engine. Ignoring the traffic signals ahead, Rousseau kept his foot planted to the floor and disappeared into the night.

THIRTY

"Thank God for that." Harris sounded relieved. "You had me worried there."

"I assume Gerard was your idea?" said Leopold, holding the telephone receiver to his ear. The study's landline was still operational, offering a more secure connection than a cell phone.

"Of course. Whatever's going on, we can't afford to take any chances. Speaking of which, I still have no idea what you're mixed up in."

"Let me worry about that."

"Same as always, huh?"

Leopold smiled. "Same as always. Listen, keep your ear to the ground. I need to know if anything comes up that's a little out of the ordinary. Can you round up the usual players?"

"Sure thing. What's your next move?"

"It's better you don't know, old friend. You've done enough. If anyone connects you to this…"

"I can take care of myself," Harris said. "Which is more than I can say about you."

"Fair point."

"Listen, I need to go. There's a board meeting I can't miss, something big. It's a great opportunity for us. I need to make sure I'm there to keep things running smoothly. I'll be back in touch, okay?"

"If I need to send any files over, I'll use Bruce," said Leopold. "Concentrate on what you need to do. And keep safe."

He hung up the phone as Mary walked into the room, her hair still damp. She wore fresh clothes taken from the wardrobes in the guest bedroom. She had the frazzled look of someone who hadn't slept in a while, but her skin was polished to a shine. Leopold smelled lilac.

"Feeling better?" he asked.

"A little," she said. "Any news from your contact on those other vics?"

"I just spoke with Harris. He's worried about me as usual. I'll send the Notre Dame files over to Bruce, a guy back in the States with access to police and government records. We should get a response soon."

"This isn't going to get me into trouble, is it?"

"Not if you don't ask me any questions about it," he said. "What did you do with your old clothes? We don't want to leave too much of a trace here, not if we can help it."

"Relax, this isn't my first rodeo. I dumped everything down the laundry chute."

"This place has a wash service?" asked Sophie.

"Most of the high end places are serviced," said Leopold. "There's usually a central room in the basement. It's a lifesaver, really."

"He gets his own laundry done and his meals brought up back at his place in New York," Mary said, looking at Sophie. "I'd be surprised if he'd ever used that fancy oven of his."

"I usually have more important things to do," he said. "Let's try to stay on topic, shall we? Until my contact comes back with any information to the contrary, we have to assume that Dubois is involved in this somehow."

"Agreed," said Mary. "And the only lead we're likely to find is going to be locked up in that giant house of his. So how do you propose we get in there?"

Leopold brought up the satellite image of the director's home. "Dubois owned a large townhouse near the Place Vauban, just south of the river. As far as we know, his wife still lives there and there's likely to be security." He tapped the screen. "The streets are largely empty of foot traffic, so the approach should be easy. But we're going to need help getting past the security."

"And what do you propose?"

Gerard appeared at the doorway. "That's where I come in."

Mary jumped. "Aren't you supposed to be keeping him out of danger, not helping him make it worse?"

"*Oui, Madame,* and the best way to protect him is to clear his name and get the police on our side. If I think we can do this without endangering his life, then we will press ahead. If not, I can arrange for him to disappear."

"I'm not going anywhere." Leopold folded his arms. "I don't run from my problems. We'll make this work, Gerard. Trust me."

"Let me take a look," said the bodyguard, joining him at the desk. "This is a wealthy neighborhood, so we should expect a security system. The easiest point of entry is here." He rapped the monitor with a knuckle. "The roof."

"I'm not convinced breaking and entering is the best way to get the police on our side," said Mary. "They tend to frown on stuff like that."

"There's not really much of a choice," said Leopold. "Without that painting, or something tying Dubois into this, I'm the only one in the picture for his murder. It doesn't matter whether the conviction sticks; if I get arrested again, I doubt I'll make it to the trial alive. This is my one chance to change that."

Mary looked him straight in the eye. "And you're sure we can pull this off?"

"I can't ask you and Sophie to come with me on this." He shook his head. "This is my mess. Gerard and I can do this alone."

"You've got to be kidding. You think this is just your mess?" Mary folded her arms. "The minute you called me from that roof top, this became my mess too, and I'll be damned if I'm backing out now."

"Same here," said Sophie. "Jean was a good man. I'm not going anywhere."

"See? I told you," said Leopold, turning to Gerard. "There's no getting rid of them. Now, how do we get inside the house?"

"There's a skylight here," said the bodyguard, pointing to the high resolution image. "That will be the weak point of entry. It will also probably be the most heavily alarmed part of the house, so we'll need to disable the security systems." He brought up a 3D image of the road outside the house. "You see here," he zoomed in. "The alarm system is made by Frontguard. That means it has a battery backup and can be controlled via cell phone."

"How do we get past it?" asked Mary.

"I have a few ideas."

"And if we get caught?"

"We call for help with this." The bodyguard held up a cell phone. "The built-in GPS is linked a central encrypted server. When your contact arranged for me to rendezvous with you here, my agency activated the chip. They can keep track of our location if I allow it." He pressed a button on the screen. "There. If we run into any serious trouble, the agency can have someone on the scene within six minutes. But I'd rather avoid the exposure. We'll attempt to get through unseen."

"How?" asked Mary.

The bodyguard slipped the phone back into his jacket pocket and smiled. "Just leave that to me."

THIRTY-ONE

The address came through. Rousseau knew the place already and kept his foot rooted to the gas pedal. Backup was primed and on the way, a full shock and awe effort complete with tactical gear. Blake wasn't going anywhere.

The Renault hit the Avenue des Champs-Élysées less than a half a mile from the target building and Rousseau slammed on the brakes. Even at this late hour there was enough traffic to make life difficult. Swearing, the police captain dropped a few gears and settled into a slow cruise, settling behind a beat-up station wagon with foreign plates. He gripped the wheel a little tighter and craned his neck for a better view. The traffic was lined up as far as he could see. He called the dispatch unit on the car phone.

"*Oui, Capitaine* Rousseau?" the phone jockey picked up on the third ring.

"I'm en route to the apartment building your guys sent through. A tactical team is also on the way. I've hit traffic. Get a message out to have them wait and meet me a block away. Find a suitable place and send me the details."

"Yes, sir."

Hanging up, Rousseau swore again and punched the wheel, sounding the horn. He saw the driver in front raise his middle finger in the mirror. Reaching across the passenger seat, the captain opened the glove box and fished out a magnetic police light. He wound down the window and fixed it to the top of the car, switching it on. The flashing siren kicked into life and the cars in front parted, exposing a narrow path down the road. Rousseau took it.

Ahead, the Arc de Triomphe glistened on the horizon, a fixed point in a sea of bustling tail lights. The captain kept his eyes on the road and pushed his right foot to the floor.

THIRTY-TWO

The restaurant was closed. Reiniger glanced through the windows as he walked past, looking for movement. The chairs outside were stacked upside down on the table tops and the ashtrays had been brought in. Keeping his head down, the assassin rounded the corner and headed for the delivery yard.

The gate was open and a single light had been left on. The dumpsters had been locked up, but the smell of old cooking was still strong. Reiniger headed for the back door and tried the handle. It was unlocked. Glad not to have to waste time picking the mechanism, the assassin stepped through to a dark hallway and followed his nose through to the kitchen, passing several doors on the way. He reached the porter's entrance and stopped.

Easing the heavy door open just a crack, Reiniger peered into the gloom and listened. An extraction fan had been left whirring, but the kitchens were otherwise silent. He walked on, his eyes adjusting to the lack of light, and headed down the galley toward the green glow of an emergency exit sign. As he drew closer, Reiniger spotted the hallway to the left and ducked inside, stepping over a small pile of vegetable peelings that hadn't been cleared away.

He spotted the old-fashioned service elevator as he rounded the corner. He pressed the call button and flinched as the machinery spluttered to life. After a few seconds, the elevator car rumbled to a halt at his feet and Reiniger reached for the handle. As his hand touched the cold metal, he froze.

A scuffling sound came from behind one of the closed doors behind him, a storage closet just off the main kitchens. He walked over and heard the noise again, faint but unmistakable. He rested one hand on the KA-BAR knife and pulled the door open.

"I'm sorry, I'm sorry!" Some kid was crouched in the corner wearing stained chef's whites. "I just needed a place to sleep, I –" he looked up. "Hey, who are you? Where's Jean-Luc?"

Reiniger moved in as the kid got to his feet. He slipped the knife out of its sheath with his right hand and used the other to force the younger man against the wall. He pressed his palm over the chef's mouth and held firm. The assassin slipped the blade between the man's legs, catching him on the inner thigh.

"Shh, shh, don't try to move," said Reiniger. "I just severed your femoral artery. You will lose blood fast, and then pass out. I promise you won't feel a thing." He smiled, looking into the kid's eyes. "It will be just like going to sleep."

The chef struggled against the German's hold, but quickly weakened. His knees gave way a few seconds later. Reiniger stepped back and let him fall to the floor, where he lay motionless. Pulling a giant roll of green paper towel from one of the shelves, the assassin staunched the growing puddle of blood that was forming on the floor and wiped the spatter off his shoes. The effect wouldn't stand up to scrutiny, but Reiniger was satisfied he was clean enough to escape a second look should someone pass him in the hallway upstairs.

Letting the door swing shut behind him, the German made his way back to the elevator and selected the sixth floor. The car rattled to a stop and he stepped out into the hallway, leaving the metal gate open. He walked toward the door that led through to the residential areas and felt for the handgun holstered beneath his suit jacket. Blake's penthouse was at the other end of the floor, with just a few apartments in between. Reiniger hoped the rest of the building's occupants were fast asleep.

Reiniger eased the door shut behind him and crept forward, scanning the area in front of his feet for any motion detectors or other equipment that might give him away. The path ahead was clear and he quickened his pace, making it halfway down the corridor before something stopped him dead in his tracks.

A distant rumble sounded ahead, coming from the stairwell. Reiniger held his breath and listened again. The noise grew louder, heavy footsteps approaching. Turning, he headed back for the elevator and ducked behind the exit door, crouching low.

He held the door open a fraction and peered out. At the end of the corridor was the stairwell door, just opposite Blake's penthouse. The noises had stopped. The assassin scanned the hallway and watched the stairwell door open, slowly at first. Next came a pair of boots, then another, and another. Half a dozen figures crept through, forming a line at the penthouse door. They wore dark uniforms, the initials 'GIPN' emblazoned on the back of their body armor, and full headgear. Each held an assault rifle, what looked like G36Ks.

How did they get here so fast? thought Reiniger, closing the door. He leaned back against the wall, his mind spinning. The GIPN, or *Groupe d'Intervention de la Police Nationale* was France's answer to the SWAT team, which meant someone back at the Commissariat wanted to make damn sure Blake found his way back into custody. With everything that had happened, that would mean a lot of loose ends for Reiniger's employer – and the assassin knew exactly what that meant for his chances of long term survival.

Letting the door shut, he glanced around the service corridor for an exit route. Riding the elevator was out of the question – the noise would immediately give away his position – and the only door led back through to the main hallway and half a dozen heavily-armed police officers. There was no way out.

He kept low and took refuge in the elevator car, sliding the metal gate closed. If anyone came looking for him, he'd still have enough time to get to the ground floor and maybe even out the back door. He hoped it didn't come to that – taking out three cops in a deserted parking lot was one thing, but an apartment block full of GIPN was pushing his luck a little too far. His only hope was to keep quiet and stay out of sight.

Reiniger pushed his back up against the wall and slowed his breathing. He listened for any signs of movement, but the only sound he could make out was his own pulse throbbing in his ears.

A brief shudder rocked the cab. Reiniger reached for the gate. It wouldn't budge. He heard the *click, click, click* of disengaging locks. With a deafening clatter, the elevator sprang to life.

THIRTY-THREE

"And you're sure this will work?" Sophie looked up. "What if you're wrong?"

Leopold sat down next to her on the sofa. "I've done the research. The alarm system is pretty high end, but it still relies on a physical telephone line. If we can find the cable, we can cut it. Then all we have to do is disable the alarm control panel inside the house."

"*J'en ai ras le bol!* Why not just let me call *Madame* Dubois? I can talk to her, maybe convince her to let me inside. Then we can find the evidence you need."

"That won't work, you know that. The police know you're involved and they'll be expecting you to make contact. Our only chance is to get in and out undetected."

"So once we've cut the telephone connection, then what?"

"The alarms will still go off if we trip any of the entry points," said Leopold. "Which means we'll need to locate and disable the control box within thirty seconds of getting inside. There's just one issue."

"And that is?"

"We have no idea where it is."

"And you don't see this as a problem?"

"Not one that's going to stop me."

"Is there anything that *would* stop you?"

Leopold opened his mouth to reply, but didn't get chance. Sophie leaned forward and put her hand on his knee.

"Why do you feel you need to run straight into danger?" she asked. "Why put yourself in harm's way? You could run, far away from here. We'd be safe."

"If I run now, I'll be running forever." He looked into her eyes and felt her hand flinch. She pulled it away.

"Don't let me interrupt," said Mary, walking in to the room.

"How long have you been standing there?" Leopold felt his face get hot and decided to change the subject. "Is Gerard ready?"

"She's got a point, you know." She looked across at Sophie. "You do have a habit of jumping in head first."

"It's worked for me so far."

"Debatable."

"About Gerard?"

Mary sighed. "He's just about ready. He asked me to bring you all through to the living room for the briefing."

"Let's go."

Gerard was waiting for them as they arrived. He stood in the middle of the floor, tie draped over a chair, his handgun holstered. "*Bon*, we are ready," he said. "We exit the building through the kitchens, the same way you came through. It's important that nobody sees us leave. Once we're outside, we can take my car to Dubois' place. It's parked around the corner."

"If we get split up?" asked Mary.

"The car is a black Mercedes CLS550. You'll find it parked along the Rue Lord Byron. There's a spare key taped to the inside of the driver's side wheel arch. If we get separated, continue with the plan. It's priority number one that we obtain the evidence from Dubois' place. *Comprenez-vous?* You understand?"

The three of them nodded.

"Good. Collect your things and shut down the computer." He looked at Leopold. "Make sure you set the hard drives to reformat. We need to wipe any trace that we were here. You'd better –" He froze in mid-sentence.

"What is it?" asked Mary.

Gerard looked at his cell phone. "We've got company. Someone tripped the motion sensors."

"That man from the parking lot?" Sophie asked.

Gerard ignored the question. "Move. Now."

As the bodyguard went for his weapon, the consultant heard a crash from the entrance hall, the sound of splintering wood. Mary instinctively reached for her hip, looking for a non-existent gun. Leopold grabbed hold of both women and pulled them back toward the study, dragging them around the corner.

"Keep down," he said, pressing his back up against the wall. He could feel his heart thumping in his chest, making him a little dizzy.

"Gerard," said Mary. "He's a sitting duck. We have to help."

Leopold peered around the corner, but couldn't see the bodyguard anywhere. Three armored figures moved cautiously through the entrance hall toward the living room, their uniforms marked with the letters "GIPN"

"I don't think they saw us," he said, turning back to Mary.

"Who the hell are they?"

"It looks like the police caught up with us sooner than we thought. I saw three of them."

"Just three?"

"There'll be more out there somewhere." Leopold inched back toward the edge of the partition wall and glanced at the empty spot Gerard had occupied seconds earlier. He scanned the room. The GIPN officers were out of sight, but the consultant could hear their footsteps on the hardwood floor. Over to the right, a shadow. Someone crouched behind one of the sofas. One of the GIPN inched closer, coming into full view. The shadow moved.

"*Hé, toi!*" Gerard drew to his full height and vaulted the sofa. Before the cop could turn around, the bodyguard was on him – one thick forearm wrapped around the man's exposed neck. His handgun drawn, Gerard used his captive as a shield and took aim at the other intruders. Leopold heard two high-pitched yelps as the bodyguard fired off his shots, both cops hitting the floor clutching at their chests.

Gerard kept his grip around the first man's throat and pulled off his helmet. Using the butt of his gun, the bodyguard knocked his opponent unconscious, letting the man's limp body fall to the carpet. Stepping over, the bodyguard made his way over to Leopold and the others. "Anyone hurt?" he asked, glancing at each of them in turn.

"No, we're fine," said Mary. "Are they dead?"

"No, but they won't be getting up anytime soon. More will be on the way soon. We need to get out of here."

"What's that sound?" said Sophie.

Leopold looked out toward the hallway. Something small and silver was rolling across the floor in their direction. It came to a rest in the middle of the living room.

"What is it?"

"Run. Now," said Gerard, pulling Leopold to his feet.

"Where to?" asked Mary. "There's no way out, in case you didn't notice."

A hissing noise.

"*Merde*! What's that?"

"Just keep moving," said Gerard, ushering the three of them toward the laundry room. "They're using smoke grenades. They'll try to disorient and separate us. Stay together." He shut the door behind him. "We've not got long."

Mary backed up against the washing machine and glared back at him. "And now we're shut up in here. Way to go, genius."

"It's a defensible position," said Gerard, holding up his gun. "And who said there was no way out?" He glanced at the laundry chute.

"You're kidding me."

"It's big enough."

"We have no idea where it goes."

"It goes to the basement. Where they collect the laundry."

"I know that. I meant, we don't know… Oh hell, never mind." Mary pulled open the hatch and looked down into the darkness. She turned to Leopold. "I officially blame you for this."

"Understood," he said.

"Let's get it over with."

THIRTY-FOUR

The elevator rumbled to a halt and Reiniger forced himself into the corner, just out of sight of the doors. His knife at the ready, the assassin watched as the metal grate slid open. A man stepped into the car and Reiniger lunged, one hand over the stranger's mouth. He used his free hand to jab the KA-BAR into the man's stomach and he doubled over, letting out a muffled groan before sliding to the floor. Reiniger brought the knife handle down hard over the man's head, knocking him out.

Looking down at the unconscious stranger, the assassin took a moment to regroup. The sleeping man was dressed in civilian clothing and smelled of expensive cologne. His shoes were clean and dry, his hair slightly damp. Other than a split lip and day-old stubble, his face was entirely unremarkable. The assassin reached down and fished inside the man's jacket pocket, locating a set of keys. The key ring read "*Appartement* 230."

Reiniger looked out into the hallway. Apartment 230 was just in view, a few feet down the corridor. He grabbed hold of the man's arms and pulled, dragging him across the carpet toward his own front door. With a brief glance to the left and right, the assassin unlocked the door and stepped through, pulling his host through after him.

Slumping the body over the sofa, Reiniger checked the rest of the man's pockets. He found a wallet, complete with driver's license, and a mobile phone. Tossing the phone, the assassin studied the ID card and slipped it into his own pocket, confident that he looked enough like the photo to use it if needed. He tossed the rest of the contents of the wallet onto the floor and made his way to the kitchen.

The apartment was small, but well furnished. The compact kitchen was fully stocked, and Reiniger helped himself to a bar of chocolate from the fridge, careful not to leave traces on any of the surfaces. He finished the entire bar in three bites, glad for the extra energy, and stuffed the empty wrapper into his pocket. A quiet moan from the living room made him look up.

"Are we awake?" Reiniger asked in French, making his way over.

The man stirred and opened his eyes. "Wh-what happened? Who are you?"

"I'm afraid it's not your turn to ask questions. You and I need to have a conversation."

"I-I'm bleeding. What's going on?"

"I don't think you're listening, *Monsieur*." Reiniger unsheathed his knife and held it up. "We're going to have a little talk. I'm going to ask you a few questions and then you're going to answer. Depending on how you behave, this doesn't have to end badly for you."

The man's eyes bulged at the sight of the blade.

"Are you listening?"

The man nodded.

"Good. The wound in your stomach is not fatal. Assuming you don't die of blood loss, you should be fine once you get to a hospital. Whether or not that happens will depend on how useful you are to me." Reiniger held the KA-BAR up to the man's face. "Now tell me, what's the best way to get out of the building without being seen?"

"Y-you take the f-fire escape to –"

"I can't use the fire escape and I can't use the main elevator. Try again."

"Th-there's another elevator on the s-second f-floor. They use it f-for disabled access. It g-goes straight to the parking lot. You can use the m-main stairs to get there."

"You have a car?"

The man nodded. "Th-the keys are over there." He pointed to a bowl near the door. "Take them, take them. They're all y-yours."

"Very good," said Reiniger, withdrawing the knife.

"I n-need an ambulance."

"We made a deal. I said you could live if you answered my questions, and you held up your end. Problem is," Reiniger leaned in closer, "I need to make sure you don't try and follow me or raise the alarm."

"I w-wont, I promise."

"And I'd like to believe you, but I'm afraid I need to be sure." The assassin thrust the KA-BAR into his host's thigh and twisted, pressing his free hand over the man's mouth.

"Try not to scream so loud," said Reiniger. "The pain will fade in a few seconds." He pulled out the knife. "You're going to start losing more blood now, but try not to move. You'll only make it worse." The assassin pulled his hand away. "Well done. Now listen carefully. Once I make it outside, I'll call for an ambulance. If I don't make it, I'm afraid you'll die here. Try to conserve your strength."

The man's eyelids flickered, his body going limp.

"Good. And don't worry, I always keep my word." Wiping the blade on the sofa, Reiniger took one last look at his host and headed for the door.

THIRTY-FIVE

Leopold hated the sensation of falling. He felt his stomach lurch as gravity took over and thrust out his hands and feet in an attempt to slow his descent. Falling from the sixth floor at full speed, even if he landed on something soft, was not part of the plan. The interior of the laundry chute was cold to the touch, but the friction quickly built up and Leopold could feel his palms burn as he slid down into the darkness. He hoped to hell he didn't land on anyone.

The laundry chute spat him out into a dumpster full of dirty clothes and he felt two pairs of hands yank him out. On his feet, Leopold blinked hard and saw the faces of Sophie and Mary come into focus in the low light.

"You all right?" Mary asked.

"Never better."

A soft *thump* announced Gerard's arrival. The bodyguard rolled out of the pile of laundry and onto his feet, pulling out his handgun. "I don't think anyone followed us," he said. "They'll figure it out soon enough, so let's keep moving."

Gerard hustled them toward the door and through into the bowels of the old building. At this time of night, the place was deserted and the only illuminations came from the dim emergency lights fixed into the ceiling. Leopold trod carefully, keeping his eyes on the silhouette of Gerard as they pressed onward. They reached the kitchens and the bodyguard held up a fist as he checked the area ahead.

"Wait here," he said. "This is where we took the elevator up to the top floor."

"So?" asked Sophie. "I don't see anything."

"Just wait here." He crept forward, both hands on his gun. He reached the metal gate and stopped. He turned around after a few seconds and walked back.

"Nothing?"

"The car must be on another floor," said Gerard. "We'll be able to hear if that changes."

"Where to now?" asked Mary.

"Back through the kitchen. Move as quietly as possible. *Bon*, stay close to me." He set off, keeping low.

The kitchen felt smaller than before. Darker, with the dormant ovens lined up against the walls, Leopold felt closed in and vulnerable. Thanks to the galley design there was nowhere to hide, just a clear line of sight. He eyed a cluster of saucepans hanging from a wall hook and wondered briefly whether a cast iron skillet would stop a bullet.

"Up ahead," said Gerard.

They reached the porter's entrance and the bodyguard edged through. Leopold followed, holding the double doors open for Sophie and Mary. Ahead, just another dark corridor.

"The back door should still be open," said Gerard. "I disabled the lock mechanism before you arrived."

They reached the exit. The bodyguard opened the door a crack and looked out.

"Can you see anything?" Mary edged forward.

"There's no road block, no cameras. It looks clear."

"Why are you saying that like it's a bad thing?" asked Sophie.

"Because if this were my show, I'd have the whole damn street locked down," said Mary. "It means whoever's in charge doesn't want word getting out. And that doesn't usually mean good things for whoever they're chasing."

"Who would have the authority?"

"Rousseau," said Leopold. "He's leading the case. He's the one with the reputation on the line. But I don't understand why he wouldn't call in the cavalry. We would have been rounded up by now." He glanced at Gerard. "No offense."

"None taken. We can talk about Rousseau later, but let's get to the car and find somewhere safe first." He stepped out into the courtyard and made his way toward the gate, checking the road outside.

"Anything?"

"No. Either someone overestimated the GIPN's abilities or this operation was deliberately under-resourced. Either way, I don't want to stick around long enough to find out which. *Allons-y.*" He waved them forward.

The air outside was warmer than before and it smelled a little damp. It was lighter too, getting close to dawn. They found the car easily enough, parked discreetly near one of the bistros on the Rue Lord Byron, a dusty back road that ran parallel to the Avenue des Champs-Élysées. Gerard waited for them to clamber inside before settling into the driver's seat next to Leopold and starting the engine.

"The target address is a few miles away, south of the river," Gerard said. "If we beat the traffic, we'll be there in ten minutes."

Leopold felt his body forced into the seat as Gerard put his foot down. The Mercedes rocketed forward with a low growl from the engine. They hit fifty miles per hour within a couple of seconds. The bodyguard slowed to take a corner and merged with the traffic on the main road back to the river, eventually settling into a moderate cruise between two taxis.

"We can access the roof via the fire escape," said Gerard. "And from there, hopefully we can disable the alarm in time. Where is the gallery located?" He aimed the question at Sophie.

"Top floor. You should see it once we get inside," she said.

"Good." Gerard turned his attention back to Leopold. "This might be our only chance. Are you ready?"

"As ready as I'll ever be."

"That will have to do."

Leopold felt the car accelerate again, Gerard guiding the sleek sedan between the cars in front. As they crossed the river, Leopold looked out across the water, black and cold. In a brief moment of weakness he wondered whether or not he'd be able to make a swim for it – then quickly pushed the thought from his mind. Whatever happened now, for better or worse, he would see it through to the end.

THIRTY-SIX

Marty Jackson, prisoner number 1537, shuffled down the corridor toward the dining hall. The other inmates from his block were lined up at the serving stations, helping themselves to Portuguese knock-off cereals and powdered milk. A few of the junkies were stocking up on bread. In a few minutes the screws would let the other blocks through, once the others got settled. There was less chance of a riot when everyone's belly was full. The big black guy the guards brought in last night was loitering at the back of the line holding an empty tray. He looked over as Marty approached but didn't say anything.

"You took off pretty fast," said Marty.

"Jerome," he replied. "You can call me Jerome."

"You're a little less uptight this morning."

"Get some breakfast." Jerome picked out a bowl and filled it with a portion of Cuétara Flakes, some kind of Portuguese cereal. "This is fresh milk?"

"The dispenser says so, but I can tell you it ain't. You wanna come down here on Thursdays. Thursdays is powdered eggs and bacon day. You get more people show up Thursdays."

"I need you to show me who runs this place. They come down for breakfast?"

Marty took a tray and filled his own bowl. "I got a good idea who you mean. Most of them are over in Block B. Should be here in a few minutes."

"I'll need an introduction."

"Not gonna happen," said Marty, helping himself to milk. "Those guys are *La Nuestra Familia*. They call the shots. If they wanna speak to you, you'll know about it."

"If someone wanted a hit carried out on the inside, they'd use those guys?"

"Why you wanna know?" Marty picked out a plastic spork and a cup of orange juice.

"Just answer the question."

"Yeah, yeah, they'd know about it," he said. "Between them and the Aryan Brotherhood, not much goes on that don't get official approval. The white boys handle the outside stuff – drugs, contraband, that sorta thing. The Spaniards handle the protection."

"Good. Where do they usually sit?"

Marty pointed at a table in the middle of the dining hall. "That one."

"Follow me."

Marty hesitated, watching his new cell mate head straight for the *Familia*'s favorite dining spot. The guy just walked over, took a seat, and started eating his cereal.

"Jesus, what are you doing?" Marty scurried over. "You wanna get us killed?"

"Relax. Sit down and eat your breakfast."

"Are you freakin' kidding me? They're letting Block B in here any second, they're gonna ask why you're sitting at their table. You got a good answer for that?"

"Sit down."

Marty did as he was told. Something in the new guy's voice forced his muscles to comply.

"Eat your breakfast," said Jerome. "Look busy. Here they come."

Looking up from his bowl, Marty saw the inmates of Block B stream into the dining hall. Like most mornings, three of the high level *Nuestra Familia* boys had shown up. They walked with swagger, displaying tattoos and muscle. The tallest, Dión, stopped dead when he saw Jerome and Marty. He pointed and muttered something in Spanish.

"C'mon, we need to get the hell out of here," said Marty.

"Just let me do the talking."

"Jesus Christ, you can't be serious."

"Be quiet."

Dión strode over, his two lieutenants close behind him, and stood at the head of the table. They looked at Jerome, then at Marty. Nobody spoke. Jerome kept crunching on his Cuétara flakes, ignoring them. Eventually, Dión slapped both palms down on the table and leaned in.

"*Amigo*, you're new here," he said. "But that don't mean you get to disrespect me and my boys in public. You need to move."

Jerome didn't look up.

"Listen, *pendejo*, I get copies of everyone's papers. I know who you are and why you're here." He glared at them both. "So don't fuck with me. I can make your

173

remaining time on this Earth very unpleasant." He paused. "Where's the other guy?"

Jerome finished his cereal and picked up the bowl, tipping the remaining milk down his throat.

"You listening to me?" said Dión.

"Yeah, I heard you," said Jerome.

"Then answer my question."

"I don't know about any other guy."

"I got papers through. Two new guys last night, one of them is you." He pointed a finger. "Where's the other."

"Your English is very good," said Jerome.

Dión looked at each of his lieutenants. "Looks like we're gonna get a workout this morning after all."

The two men folded their arms and smirked.

"The only thing I'm having trouble *working out*," said Jerome, getting to his feet, "is how you got papers through for a prisoner that never made it onto the bus. I'm sure you've got a good story."

Dión and his men all stood well over six feet four inches tall, but Jerome still had a considerable height advantage. One of the lieutenants took an instinctive step backward.

"How about we sit down and have a conversation," Jerome continued. "And you can tell me where you get your orders." He stared down at Dión, who didn't flinch. "Or does this have to get messy?"

"Look around you, *cabrón*." The gang leader tilted his head. "You think you got any say in what goes on around here? You see those four C.O.s?" He glanced at the guards pacing the perimeter of the room. "They ain't gonna help you none. Ain't nobody in here can touch me, ain't nobody gonna blink an eyeball if I gut

174

you right here, right now. Maybe we just cut you up a little and see what the warden says when I tell him you tryin' to get in my way. What you think, boys?"

The two minions grinned, exposing yellow teeth.

Jerome smiled. "The warden, huh? You guys talk often?"

Dión's smile faded.

"And here's me thinking the criminals I've met on the *outside* are dumb," said Jerome. "I never even thought about the ones stupid enough to get caught."

Marty saw the muscles in Dión's arms tense. The other two men stepped forward.

"I think it's time we got the warden's attention, don't you?" Jerome glanced down at Marty.

"Don't bring me into this."

"Relax, just concentrate on being a reliable witness."

"Witness to what?"

"These three little ladies getting sent to the infirmary."

There came a blur and Marty flinched. He saw Dión thrust something at Jerome's stomach with a short, sharp jab. Jerome caught the gang leader's wrist and twisted, lashing out at Dión's nose with his other hand. He hit the Spaniard hard, crushing the nasal bridge.

Dión dropped whatever weapon he was holding and Jerome pushed him backward into one of his buddies, sending both men toppling to the floor. Grabbing the third gang member by the shoulders, Jerome brought his forehead down hard, hitting the shorter man in the face. Marty couldn't see what had happened, but there was a loud crunching sound and the second lieutenant went down, clearly out of commission.

The first lieutenant recovered, shoving the groaning Dión off him and onto the tiles. He jumped to his feet and lunged, something sharp in his hand. With one fluid movement, Jerome caught the man's arm and aimed a jab at the throat. The gang member choked as the blow hit home, clutching at his larynx with his free hand. Jerome finished with a fist to the jaw, knocking his opponent flat on his back. He didn't get up again.

"That should do it," said Jerome, turning to Marty. "Just make sure you get us a meeting with the warden. Tell him we want to make a deal, or something. You can just make it up. He'll be curious enough to see what we know."

Marty saw three guards sprinting in their direction, drawing Tasers. They were shouting something in French.

"I hate this part," said Jerome.

One of the guards fired his weapon, hitting Jerome in the chest. The needles dug into his flesh, connected to the handset by a length of thin wire. There was a fizzing noise and Jerome tensed, his teeth clamped shut. Another guard fired and Jerome fell to his knees, his face screwed up in pain.

Then he passed out.

THIRTY-SEVEN

After cutting the external telephone line, Gerard led them up to the roof of Jean Dubois' grand townhouse and examined the skylight. The early morning sunshine made the job easier and it wasn't long before he'd found a way through. Pulling out a short knife hidden near his ankle, Gerard unscrewed the hinges that held the frame in place and waved Leopold over.

"*Regardez*, once I remove the pane, we'll have thirty seconds to deactivate the alarm. We don't have the code, so you'll need to pull out the power line from the main circuit. You can use this," he handed Leopold the knife. "Force the panel open with the blade and cut the blue wire."

"You've done your homework," said Mary. "But why him?"

"He can move quicker than I can."

"Where's the panel?" asked Sophie.

Gerard smiled. "Most people expect forced entry through the front door, so they install the alarm box as far away as possible. Look." He pointed. "Near the top of the stairs. Just don't make any noise. If there are any security guards they could radio for assistance."

Leopold nodded.

"I'll be watching from here. If you get into any trouble, I'll pull you out." He pulled open the skylight and held it up.

The consultant eyed Gerard's thick arms and didn't doubt his promise. Crouching, Leopold sidled over the edge of the open window and eased himself down until he was hanging by his arms. He let go and dropped the final few feet, bending his knees as he hit the carpet. He landed silently. The upstairs hallway was dark and empty, and he could make out a series of corridors leading off to other parts of the house.

Moving over to the alarm panel at the top of the stairs, Leopold jammed the blade between the lid and pried the box open, exposing a circuit board. He noticed a chunky battery and a mass of wires. Spotting the blue lead running from the battery, he severed the cord and tensed, half expecting the alarms to sound.

Nothing happened.

His grip on the knife relaxing slightly, Leopold turned and made his way back to the skylight and waved the others down. Gerard lowered Mary and Sophie to the carpet before jumping down himself.

"The gallery is this way," said Sophie, heading for one of the corridors.

"I'll go in front," said Gerard, holding up his hand. "Let's hope the lady of the house is asleep."

The bodyguard stepped up and led them through into the gloomy hallway, where Leopold spotted a crack of light toward the back wall.

"There," said Sophie. "Behind the door. Someone's left the lights on."

Gerard reached the door and paused, apparently listening out for any sound of movement beyond. With a curt nod, he eased the door open, flooding the corridor with light. Leopold stepped through behind him, blinking hard as his eyes adjusted.

"Wow, this place is not quite what I expected," said Mary.

Leopold couldn't agree more. A large, circular room, not significantly smaller than a modest Paris apartment in its own right, waited for them. Hung from its walls were several dozen paintings of various sizes and styles, each presented in a gilded frame and individually lit by wall-mounted bulbs. A small brass plaque beneath each announced the artist and title, and in the center of the room stood a backless wooden bench, positioned to allow the sitter an unobstructed view of any part of the gallery.

"I don't see 'The Virgin Mary with Saint Anne'," said Sophie. "He must have hidden it. But there's nowhere in here I can think of that would make a good hiding place."

"That's because you're only seeing what's right in front of you," said Leopold. "We have to think like Jean Dubois. Figure out what he would do."

"How do we do that?"

"Jean Dubois was not exactly a criminal mastermind." Leopold walked over to one of the paintings and inspected the frame. "But he was smart enough to know that entrusting the Da Vinci to anyone else would have been a fatal mistake. He would have hidden it in this house somewhere. And he wouldn't have wanted to get his family involved."

"Jean loved his family," said Sophie. "He'd never do anything to hurt them."

"Which means he would hide the painting somewhere nobody else in the house would look. And what better place than here, in his own private sanctuary?" He ran a finger along the frame and smiled.

"But where exactly?"

Leopold stood in front of the painting, an original Dominico Morelli. "This seems to be roughly the right size, doesn't it?" he said.

"I don't understand."

"This piece is the center of Dubois' collection. I guess his favorite." He lay the painting on the floor, face down. He pulled out the knife.

"What are you doing?" asked Sophie, stepping forward.

"This is the only frame that's the right size," he said. Without waiting for a response, Leopold slipped the knife between the frame and the backing, slicing open the protective tape.

"Be careful, don't damage it."

Leopold ignored her and peeled away the brown paper fastened to the inside of the frame. Tearing away the last of the tape, he felt his heart skip.

"What's that?" asked Sophie, kneeling down next to Leopold.

"Ladies and gentlemen," he looked up. "I give you our missing painting." With a grin, he held up "The Virgin and Child with Saint Anne".

"You're kidding me," said Mary. "People were killed for this? I don't get what the big deal is."

"That's not surprising. Most people don't know a good thing when they see it," said Sophie.

"And what's that supposed to mean?"

"Never mind."

"No, go on, enlighten me."

"Can we do this later?" said Leopold. He turned his attention to the painting. "Oil on wood, very fragile. We can't transport it without a protective case or it might fall to pieces. I'll need to take some photos and leave the original here."

"Use this," said Mary, handing over her cell phone. "You should get a high enough resolution for what you need."

"Good. We can upload the photos to the web. Hopefully, Rousseau will get the hint."

"He's not exactly going to call this whole thing off on the basis of one photo," said Mary. "He'll need to do some digging. That could take days."

"But it should be enough to cast doubt," said Leopold, lining up the camera and taking a handful of shots. "Which gives us our first advantage. We've got the details on the black sedan that was following you, the fake I.D., and I'm guessing they've found camera footage of the shootout in the parking lot by now. If we can find just one connection between the other shooting victims, something that links them to Dubois, then we've got enough evidence to stay out of jail. We can arrange for the US embassy to take us in until then."

"Finally, you're starting to make sense. You done with that?" she held out her hand.

"Let me hang on to this for now," said Leopold, slipping the handset into his jacket. "You're not going anywhere, are you?"

"Not while you've got my phone."

"We should seal this back up," said Gerard, moving closer. "We have what we came for. If we stay here any longer, we might run into Mme. Dubois. I expect she'll be sleeping lightly after recent events."

A faint noise at the doorway caught Leopold's attention. Gerard heard it too and reached for his holster.

"I wouldn't worry about the old lady." A figure swept through the door, dressed in a charcoal suit and holding a gun in both hands. "She took her late husband's advice and left town two days ago." The accent was German.

Gerard froze, his back to the intruder. He rested one hand on his weapon.

"Don't do that." The figure stepped into the light. He met Leopold's stare. "I see you remember me. So you know what I'm capable of. I had hoped to catch up with you at the apartment, but, unfortunately the police beat me to it."

The consultant saw Gerard tense, his eyes flicking to the right. A signal? Leopold couldn't be sure.

"I'll need you to pass me the cell phone, please." The German held out a hand. "Bring it to me."

Leopold didn't move. "How did you find us?"

"Bring me the cell phone."

"It won't do you any good. I've already uploaded the photographs."

The intruder pursed his lips. "That was an error, Mr. Blake. Those photographs were the only thing keeping you alive. As it stands, I have no more need for any of you." He brought the gun up and aimed.

Gerard chose that moment to attack. Spinning on his back leg, he aimed a kick to the intruder's face. The German saw it coming and dodged to the side, narrowly avoiding contact. Gerard span, bringing his other foot around as his opponent regained his footing. The bodyguard's blow hit home, forcing the German back toward the door. The bodyguard lifted his firearm and took aim, but the intruder was too fast, dodging inside the larger man's reach and rolling out of harm's way, gun still in his hand.

Gerard whipped around, bringing his own weapon to bear. The intruder feinted, stepping to the side as Gerard moved in. He grabbed the bodyguard's arm and wrenched it backward, simultaneously aiming a kick to the knee. Gerard buckled. The German lifted his handgun and aimed in Mary's direction.

"Down!" Leopold dived, tackling her to the floor. Sophie followed suit.

The intruder hesitated for a split second, apparently trying to choose a target. The momentary lapse in concentration gave Gerard the opportunity to free his arm. He aimed a jab to his opponents throat, causing the other to stumble as he tried to avoid contact.

Lunging from his crouching position, the bodyguard tackled the smaller man, sending them both crashing into the wall. Leopold heard a *crunch* of glass and wood as several frames splintered and fell to the floor. Gerard jabbed at the German's stomach, knocking the wind out of him. The intruder grunted and twisted, bringing up a knee. Gerard blocked with his forearm, dropping his gun.

"Get out of here!" Gerard ordered.

The words took a second or two to hit home. Leopold's brain kicked into action and he grabbed hold of Mary's wrist.

"We need to go," he said.

"You don't need to tell me twice." She tugged at Sophie's arm. "Come on, I think we can make it to the door."

"I'll try and give Gerard a hand. Maybe buy us all some time."

Sucking in a deep breath, Leopold let go of Mary and sprang to his feet, diving at the two men. He lowered his shoulder and went for the German's legs, lifting the man up into the air. Out of the corner of his eye, he saw Mary and Sophie reach the door. He felt a dizzying pain across the top of his skull and toppled to the ground, grasping his crown in both hands. He felt something warm and wet. Was that blood? Looking up, he saw the intruder shove Gerard backward a couple of feet. The bodyguard stumbled, trying not to trip over Leopold.

Then came the shot.

Ears ringing, Leopold didn't register the sound at first. In close quarters, the noise of a gun firing was deafening. He patted himself down, feeling his chest for any signs of an entry wound. There was nothing. He looked around and saw that Mary and Sophie had managed to get out.

Then he realized what had happened.

THIRTY-EIGHT

Gerard fell to his knees, blood pooling on his shirt. The German brought the gun up again, aiming for Leopold this time. Gerard grunted and lunged forward, shoving the smaller man back against the wall.

"I've got this," said Gerard. "Get out. Now. Take the car and get the others away. Go!"

Leopold blinked hard, still dizzy from the pistol-whip to the head, and got to his feet. He felt a little shaky.

"Now!"

The German recovered, knocking Gerard back to his knees. Leopold rushed toward the door, slamming it shut behind him. Mary and Sophie were crouched a few feet down the hallway. He heard another shot and ducked, half-expecting a bullet to punch through the wood above his head.

Then silence.

"We need to get out of here," he said, breathing heavily. "Follow me to the car."

"What about Gerard?" asked Sophie.

Leopold felt a pang of remorse in his chest. He shook his head. "There's nothing we can do. Please, we need to get out of here." He broke into a jog.

"How the hell did that guy find us?" said Mary, following close behind.

"Is that the man from the parking lot?" asked Sophie.

"Just keep moving."

The trio reached the stairs and Leopold grabbed the railing, taking the steps two at a time. They hit the ground floor without breaking stride and Mary reached the front door first. Her hands a blur, she slid open the chains and locks, throwing the door wide open.

The light was dazzling. Now fully risen, the sun bathed the streets in a white glow, making Leopold's eyes sting as he jogged out into the road. The Mercedes was parked nearby, just across the street. They reached the car and Leopold fumbled under the wheel arch, locating the spare key. He opened the doors and climbed inside.

"What are you waiting for?" asked Mary, buckling up in the front passenger seat.

"How the hell did he track us here?" said Leopold. "Unless he got to the computer back at the apartment..." He pulled out Mary's cell phone from his jacket pocket. "But that would have been impossible with the GIPN in the building."

"Unless one of Rousseau's men is involved?"

"There's only one way to find out." He dialed a number on the phone's keypad and hung up almost immediately. He opened the car door and tossed the cell phone onto the sidewalk. "Hey, what the hell?" said Mary. "That's a brand new phone."

"I'll get you another." He started the car and turned around, heading away from the river. "Just trust me."

"Trust you?"

He turned to face her. "It's just a phone."

"You just left Gerard in there to die."

"There's nothing we could do, Mary. He used whatever strength he had left to get us out of there. We're alive thanks to him. I'll make sure the person behind this gets everything they deserve."

"And I'm supposed to just trust your judgment on that? You don't even know what's going on in your own company. How can I trust that you know what's going on here?"

"Is this really the right time?" asked Sophie from the back seat. "I think I can hear police sirens. Maybe we should –"

"Stay out of this," said Mary. "I'm serious," she continued, turning back to Leopold.

"What are you talking about?"

"My sister called."

"Your sister? I thought you two didn't speak." He turned a corner and hit the main road.

"Well, she's taken it upon herself to stick her nose into my business. And that means sticking her nose into your business, it seems. You know anything about a chemical research division at Blake Investments?"

He looked at her. "Sure. Why?"

"The WHO are looking into it."

Leopold didn't reply.

"You really don't have any clue what's going on?"

Leopold put his foot down and changed lanes. "I get a quarterly report. What's this got to do with anything?"

Mary sighed. "You don't think it's strange that someone would go out of their way to stage such an elaborate way of keeping you out of the picture? They could have just hired someone to pick you off. Why do you think that is?"

"Because maybe it's just not enough to kill me."

"Listen, Leopold. My sister told me she's got someone on the inside. Someone working at your chemical research division. She said they've discovered something that could prove to be very dangerous in the wrong hands."

"What else did she say?"

"She said the WHO first noticed issues after the division shut itself off from the public. They thought the researches might have discovered something they didn't want anyone to know about."

"When was this?"

"Three years ago."

Leopold gripped the steering wheel a little harder.

"What is it?" asked Mary.

He turned to look at her. "Three years ago, after nearly half a decade of zero progress, I was forced to step back from the division. The EU passed new regulations making it illegal for any private organization in the research sectors to have any ties to military suppliers."

"And Blake Investments owns a few of those, I suppose?"

"I was allowed to own shares in the company, I just wasn't allowed to run it. Apparently, it was supposed to prevent any conflicts of interest."

"So?"

"So, I had to sever all ties with the company and hand the reins over. That included preparing a trust deed that allowed for an executor to use my shares to vote on my behalf if anything ever happened to me."

"Let me guess – like if you were killed?"

"Or found unfit to act. Which includes –"

"Getting arrested for murder," said Mary.

"Potentially, yes. The board only needs a reasonable excuse to trigger the transfer of my voting rights to my executor." He slapped his palm down on the dash, making Sophie jump. "Find the motive, find the killer." He turned to Mary. "It's been staring me in the face all this time."

"It's circumstantial, at best," she said. "We'll need proof."

Leopold undertook a slow-moving van ahead, eliciting a series of enraged blasts from the driver's horn. "What about this for proof? How do you think the German managed to track us to the apartment and then to Dubois' house?"

"Maybe there's a leak in Rousseau's unit," said Mary.

"Not likely. Remember what Gerard told us? About if we needed extraction?"

"His agency can track him via his cell phone. You think it's someone at the agency?"

"Think about the motive," said Leopold. "What if someone intercepted Gerard's cell signal and sent it somewhere else? It would be easy enough to do, if you knew what you were doing."

"But how would they know which signal to trace?"

"There is one way," said Leopold. "If you already know which cell phone to look for."

THIRTY-NINE

"What do you think he wants with us?" Rose's voice was a whisper, barely audible over the background noise from The *Thanatos'* engines. "Do you think he knows anything?"

Following their impromptu sleepover, James had suggested they grab a bite to eat from the ship's mess hall before the breakfast rush. Before they could even grab a slice of toast, one of the stewards had shown up and ordered them to report to the Director's office. Immediately.

"It's probably nothing," said James, leading the way down the long corridor. "Maybe one of the projects I've got you and your team working. You've turned out some pretty impressive results recently." He wasn't sure who he was trying to convince.

"I'll take that as a compliment after last night," she said, nudging him, any trace of concern now gone.

"Speaking of which, don't let anybody know about us," he said. "You know the policy."

"Yeah, yeah, I know. Kinda makes it more fun though, right?"

James pulled open the door at the end of the hallway. "You're going to be trouble, aren't you? I can tell."

"You ain't seen nothing yet." She breezed through. "Boss."

James shook his head and followed, catching up with a few long strides. Rose increased her pace too, taunting him. He laughed, a little louder than intended, and tugged at her arm. She turned, and James pushed her up against the wall.

"Don't tempt me," he said.

"Now's probably not the best time."

"I guess not," he pulled away.

"I'll come visit later." She leaned in and planted a kiss on his cheek. "Just so long as you behave yourself."

"Deal."

They rounded the corner and made their way up the narrow staircase to the top deck, where a set of double doors manned by a pair of security guards blocked their path. The doors were double height, as were the guards, and one of them held up a giant palm as the two operatives approached.

"Arms out to your sides, please." The slightly larger of the two stepped forward and patted James' clothes, apparently checking for weapons or recording devices.

"Ma'am." The other guard repeated the process with Rose.

Satisfied, the larger guard swiped a key card across a magnetic reader and the doors slid open. He beckoned them forward and led them through to a cavernous office while the other remained on duty outside. The doors slid closed.

"Wait here," said the guard, disappearing into a side room.

James looked around. The Director's office was easily the largest on the ship, with high ceilings and plate glass windows that looked out across the bow toward the horizon. In the early morning sunlight, the view was breathtaking. Aside from an expansive desk, a drinks cabinet, a few chairs, and a number of wall mounted LCD monitors, the room was empty. The soft carpet, a rich blue color, matched the hue of the ocean almost perfectly.

"This place gives me the creeps," said Rose. "God only knows what goes on up here."

"Relax, we'll be out of here soon enough."

"I hope you're right."

James looked at Rose, registering the note of concern in her voice. He squeezed her hand. "We'll be back below deck in no time. You better start thinking about our next sleepover."

She squeezed his hand back. "I'll try not to get too distracted."

Rose let go as the guard re-entered the room, followed by a tall man in a dark suit. James recognized him as the Director, although he seemed a little thinner than James remembered. The Director took a seat behind the desk.

"Please, sit down," he said, as the guard brought over two chairs. "Do you know why you're here?"

The two operatives obliged, settling into their seats. James felt the shadow of the security guard fall across his back, making the hairs on his neck stand on end.

"No, sir," said James. He glanced at Rose.

The Director leaned forward. His face was hard and angular, as though sculpted from rock. His eyes were dark, almost black, and there were faint scars around his forehead and chin.

"No, sir." Rose shook her head.

"You spoke with one of the technicians yesterday. Asked him to trace some electronic payments for you." The Director paused. "Why?"

James coughed. "Just following up on a lead, sir."

"I trust you got the results you were looking for?"

"Yes, sir," said Rose. "We're getting really close now."

"Good, good." He nodded at the security guard who was standing somewhere near the back of the room. "Although the technician in question had a slightly different story."

James felt movement behind him and tensed up. The security guard crossed the floor and positioned himself behind Rose's chair. He grabbed hold of Rose's head in both hands and twisted hard, wrenching her head backward. James heard a sickening *crack* as the guard snapped her neck like a twig. He began to hyperventilate.

"Disloyalty is a cancer that can spread quickly," said the Director. "One has to destroy it at the source before it gets chance."

James' instinct was to jump to his feet, but his muscles weren't responding. He was rooted to his chair, unable to move. The guard let go of Rose's head and her body fell forward, toppling from the chair and onto the floor. James felt his stomach lurch.

"You really should have known better, Mr. Cullen," the Director continued. "I had high hopes for you." He opened a desk drawer and pulled out a large syringe, laying it down in front of him. "Do you know what this is?"

James shook his head, unable to speak.

"It's something we've been working on. In small doses, it can be used as a muscle relaxant. In slightly higher doses, test cases have been known to experience feelings of euphoria. We anticipate quite a market for this one." He held the syringe in one hand and studied it. "In heavy doses, it causes the body to shut down. Unfortunately for our animal test subjects, this ultimately resulted in death by asphyxiation. We've not been able to secure any human trials yet."

James felt the security guard grab hold of his arms, forcing him to keep still.

"Which is where you come in," said the Director. He stood up, syringe in hand, and stepped over Rose's body. Taking hold of James' sleeve, he rolled it up to expose the skin. "This might hurt."

A jolt of pain shot through James' arm as the needle punctured his flesh and the Director emptied the contents of the syringe into his blood stream. The security guard let go. James tried to get to his feet, but his legs wouldn't respond.

"How are you feeling?"

James couldn't have replied, even had he wanted to. He felt gravity take hold and toppled forward, his abdominal muscles unable to keep his torso upright. Slipping off the chair, he hit the carpet and rolled onto his side. Unable to move his head, he could only look ahead. Rose stared back at him, her eyes dull and empty. He held her gaze.

"I'm sorry it had to come to this," said the Director, his voice somewhere above. "But I trust you'll both be very happy together." The voice trailed off.

Although all life had left Rose's body, in the moments before James died he was certain he saw her smile.

FORTY

"Here," said Sophie, handing her cell phone to Leopold. "Please don't throw this one out the window."

He thanked her and turned his attention to the Mercedes' onboard computer. Punching in a code, he synced the phone to the car's hands free system and dialed a number from memory.

"And you're sure it's him?" asked Mary.

"It can't be anyone else," said Leopold. The call connected and began to ring through. "This ends now."

A voice answered. *"Bonjour, comment puis-je vous aidez?"*

"I'm afraid to report we're still alive," said Leopold. "And your options are running out. Call your man off."

"Leopold? Is that you? Are you okay?"

"Drop the act, Harris."

"What are you talking about?"

"You must have known we'd figure it out eventually," Leopold continued. "Otherwise you'd have let the police take us down."

"I don't know what –"

"You were the one who sent Gerard. You knew he'd activate the tracer, so you arranged an intercept."

"What are you talking about? Why would I want to –"

"I know about Chemworks," said Leopold. "With me out of the way, you get full control. I trusted you."

"What about Chemworks? That business is a dog. I've barely heard from them in months."

Leopold turned to Mary and nodded.

"Not according to the WHO," she said. "Oh, and by the way, next time you send someone after me, tell them not to follow so close. You think I can't smell a tail?"

"I have people looking into your movements over the last few months, Harris," said Leopold. "They'll find something that ties you to this. You can't run."

The line was silent.

"Let's end this now," said Leopold. "You've got nowhere left to go."

"They won't find anything," said Harris, "because there is nothing to find. And who are they going to believe? Me, a respected member of the business community, or a disgraced playboy billionaire who's wanted for murder? I doubt the board will have any issues in following my recommendations."

"What recommendations?"

"You handed the company over to me three years ago. You gave me this worthless job, on top of my regular duties, which, by the way, you don't pay me *nearly* enough for. Well, Chemworks has a real shot of making some actual revenue. We just need some outside investment, that's all. And I'm the one who's going to make it happen."

"Harris, what are you doing? You can't let that research fall into the wrong hands," said Mary.

"There's nothing more to discuss," said Harris. "I'm recommending the sale of the company, including

Leopold's shares, to an outside investor – for twelve times their current value. Given the circumstances, I doubt the board will refuse."

"Don't do it," said Leopold. "You don't know what will happen. They'll have full control."

"I know. I'm the one who drafted the contracts," said Harris. "Perhaps if you hadn't gotten yourself arrested for murder… I wouldn't be forced to take such drastic action."

"Bullshit," said Mary.

"I don't know what you're talking about. Besides, there's nothing you can do about it now. All I need is the board to vote on this. I'll have an answer within the hour."

"We're coming for you, Harris," said Leopold. "I'm not going to let this happen."

"I look forward to seeing you," he replied. "You know where to find me."

With a burst of static, the line went dead.

"We need to get to the La Defense office," said Leopold, planting his right foot to the floor. "We've got less than an hour. If Chemworks has found something *that* valuable, it can't be anything good."

The engine roared as the twin turbos pumped more air into the combustion chamber, forcing the car forward. The speedometer nudged ninety miles per hour.

"He'll call the police," said Sophie. "We can't go after him."

"He won't," said Leopold, weaving in and out of the slower traffic. "He'll want to keep us quiet."

"He'll use the German."

The consultant nodded. "Right. Which means we're going to need a little help."

FORTY-ONE

Prison Warden Jean Guinault's office was smaller than Marty had expected, and messy as hell. Stacks of paper covered every available surface and the trash can looked like it hadn't been emptied in weeks. Marty sat in a cheap plastic chair, hands cuffed together, watching the warden pace the room. The old man wore a suit, but he'd tossed the jacket somewhere and his tie was halfway undone. His shirt sleeves were rolled up, exposing thick forearms. After a few minutes of waiting, there came a knock at the door and the warden pulled it open.

"*Allez*, bring him in" said Guinault, sticking his head through the doorway. A uniformed guard entered, followed by Jerome, whose hands were cuffed behind his back.

"Thank you. Leave us now."

"Sir?" The guard looked puzzled. "This man took out three *Familia* with his bare hands. You shouldn't be left alone with –"

"I can handle this myself, get out." The warden ushered the C.O. out of the room, locking the door behind him. He turned to look at Jerome. "Please, take a seat."

Jerome sat down next to Marty, straining the chair.

"That was quite a stunt you pulled in the cafeteria," said Guinault. "It's safe to say you have my attention."

"Good," Jerome said.

"We can speak freely here, I've made sure nobody will disturb us. But be very aware," the old man stepped forward, "one wrong move, I'll throw you back to the wolves."

"I'm not interested in the wolves, we're here to talk about you. Specifically, why you ordered *La Nuestra Familia* to take me out."

If the warden was surprised, he didn't show it. "I hear you've had trouble with our Spanish friends. Why is this my problem?"

"You've met Dión?"

"I've had the unfortunate pleasure of meeting most of the inmates here."

"Then you'll know Dión isn't exactly the sharpest shank in the cell block," said Jerome. "And the idea of him getting ahold of stolen prisoner transfer papers doesn't sound right to me."

"Get to the point."

"He must have had help. I'm guessing you know something about that."

The warden's face twisted. "I think you're forgetting where you are. You have no power here, no friends. I was prepared to help you out," he leaned in close, getting right in Jerome's face. "But you can just rot in here, for all I care."

Marty nearly jumped out of his chair as Jerome kicked out and hit the warden in the knee. There was a crunching sound where the warden's kneecap and cartilage were crushed together and Guinault flopped forward onto his front with a yelp of pain. Before he could get up, Jerome was out of the chair, his legs wrapped around the warden's neck.

"Let's try this another way," said Jerome, his hands still cuffed behind his back. "I'm going to keep squeezing until you give me an answer I'm happy with." He applied extra pressure and the warden groaned, arms thrashing at his side. "If you don't play ball, I'll make sure to crush your larynx before snapping your neck. Just to make sure you get my point."

"Jesus Christ, what the hell are you doing?" said Marty, getting to his feet. "We won't make it through the night if anything happens to him."

The warden's eyes were bulging out of his head, but he appeared to be nodding.

Jerome grinned. "Warden Guinault is going to cooperate and everything is going to work out. Aren't you?" He squeezed a little tighter and the old man slapped a palm down on the carpet. Jerome eased off a little. "I thought so."

"You're insane," said Marty. "Jesus Christ, you're completely insane. What exactly are you expecting him to tell you?"

"He's going to tell me who's pulling the strings. Somebody went to a lot of trouble to make sure I wound up here, and the only way they could have arrange it all is to go through official channels." He relaxed his hold a little more. "So, *Monsieur*, shall we start at the beginning?"

Guinault gurgled something incomprehensible.

"You might have to repeat that," said Jerome.

"And you think he's just going to let us walk out of here?" said Marty.

"Of course."

"Why the hell would he do that?"

"Because once the other prison staff get involved, this whole mess goes public. He can't tell anyone, or else he'll implicate himself."

"What about *La Nuestra Familia*?"

Jerome smiled. "I'll be out of here soon enough. In the meantime, my recent bad behavior has gotten me a stretch in solitary. A few days in the SHU ought to keep me out of trouble."

Marty rubbed his temples. "You make it sound like you had this planned all along."

"Maybe I did."

The warden slapped his palm on the carpet again and mumbled something Marty couldn't quite make out.

"Ready to talk?" asked Jerome.

The warden nodded.

"Good. Let's get started, shall we?"

FORTY-TWO

There was blood everywhere. Captain Rousseau studied the scene, stepping over the tiny orange markers the forensics team had dotted around the floor. The room was some kind of private art gallery, although some of the paintings now sat at odd angles. One or two of them had broken frames, the glass splintered and cracked. More troubling than that, the body of a man dressed in an expensive suit was leaking blood all over the floor.

The attempted extraction at the penthouse had been a monumental failure, but at least they'd caught up with Blake before he'd had a chance to wipe the computers. Unfortunately, the commissioner was unlikely to see the silver lining, especially now there was yet another dead body to account for. This latest murder brought the body count up to seven – that he knew about.

"Cause of death was a gunshot wound to the chest," said the medical examiner, standing over the body. "Massive internal hemorrhaging soon followed. Nothing anybody could have done."

"Any prints?"

"Defensive wounds to the face and arms. We might be able to pull some DNA, but I doubt it. Whoever took this guy out must have been a professional."

"What makes you say that?"

"There's a second bullet wound, a non-fatal injury. Somehow, this man kept on fighting even though he had been shot. Just looking at him I can tell he has combat training."

"Meaning whoever killed him had better training," said Rousseau. "*Bon*, find what you can. Get me an ID on the victim and how he links up with this whole mess. I'll be outside."

The medical examiner nodded and Rousseau left the room, heading for the stairs. He reached the ground floor and stopped to catch his breath.

"*Capitaine! Ici!*" The rookie's shouts came from outside.

Rousseau scowled and made his way over.

"*Capitaine*, I found something," the cop said, pointing at the floor.

Rousseau paused. He pulled on a pair of latex gloves and got to his knees. Lying on the sidewalk, a cell phone. "Anything else?"

"Witnesses say there was a black Mercedes parked here earlier, not a car they recognized. Maybe they dropped this."

Or maybe not, thought Rousseau, picking the device up with a gloved hand. "Dismissed," he said. The rookie shuffled off.

The captain unlocked the screen and checked the call history. The last call was made less than thirty minutes ago. He dropped the phone into a Ziploc bag and waved one of the forensic technicians over.

"*Oui, Capitaine?*"

"Here, take this," he handed the bag over. "Get me a trace on the last number dialed. I also want you to clone this handset and forward all incoming messages and calls to me. Understand?"

The tech nodded.

"Good. You've got twenty minutes." He waved with the back of his palm. "Get moving, please."

The tech walked off back to the apartment block and handed the Ziploc bag to one of the juniors working the front door. Rousseau headed back to his car and climbed in, shutting out the noise from the street. He started the engine and rolled the car out onto the main road, drumming his fingers against the steering wheel as he made his way back to the station.

FORTY-THREE

Reiniger rested his hand on his gun and tried to resist the temptation to use it. Harris looked angry, and that was hardly unexpected, but the assassin knew that raised tempers weren't going to solve anything. If the man would only take a break and put things into perspective... The assassin abandoned that line of thinking. By now, his own chances of a favorable outcome were dwindling by the second, but maybe Harris had a point. Maybe Blake really *was* dumb enough to force a confrontation.

"I want that asshole strung up by his neck," said Harris. "I want to watch him die. You know how long I've put up with his bullshit?"

"Twenty years," said Reiniger.

"That's damn right. Twenty years of service and he gives me, what, fucking Chemworks? What the hell else was I supposed to do?"

The assassin didn't reply.

"There *was* nothing else to do. And if a few people have to suffer along the way, then... screw 'em! It's about time I got what's coming to me. And who's really getting hurt here? Blake? He's no angel, you know."

Reiniger nodded, his patience wearing thin.

"And you never met his father. Talk about fruit falling from the tree. If you ask me, the world's better off with both of them dead. They deserve worse."

"Do you have orders." Reiniger didn't phrase it as a question.

Harris looked up. "The deal is done. There's nothing Blake can do to stop that now. But there's no point me making all this money if Blake gets the police on his side – I can't enjoy it from prison, can I?"

The assassin didn't reply.

"Blake will make his way to us. He's too damn proud to run, and that'll be his downfall. He'll charge in here just like always, expecting to get his own way. And we'll be waiting."

"We should clear the building."

"Nonsense. This is the company's busiest European office. We can't just close it down without drawing attention."

"I can't do my job with this many people around," said Reiniger.

"Sure you can. You're a resourceful guy, find a way."

The assassin grunted. "There will be witnesses."

"Then be careful. This is your last chance to fix this. If the police get to Blake first we're all dead men. I wasn't kidding when I said this was a one-way ticket – retirement can mean two things in this line of work, remember that."

Reiniger bit his tongue. "Make sure the security teams are alerted."

"Already have. The front desk and surveillance teams have been briefed. Every square inch of this place is covered by security cameras, except this office, of course. If Blake, or any of the others, get within fifty feet of here, we'll know about it."

"The only points of entry are on the ground floor," said Reiniger, turning to leave. "I'll wait for them there. Have the security team patch me in to their radio."

Harris nodded and the assassin left the room, closing the door firmly behind him. The top floor of the office building, where Harris kept his office, was used largely by the finance teams that kept this particular division of Blake Investments in the black. The area was busy; dozens of young interns carried stacks of paper between offices, while older executives barked orders from behind their desks. All around, the floor-to-ceiling glass offered views of La Defense from twenty stories high.

His head down, Reiniger made his way to the stairwell and began the long descent to the ground floor. Taking the steps two at a time, his pulse rate barely elevated, he fitted the custom sound suppressor to his firearm and tucked the weapon back into its holster. He buttoned up his suit jacket, trying to conceal the bulge, and slipped a transparent communication bud into his ear canal.

After a few seconds of static the signal cleared and he was synced in to the building's security chatter. With over three hundred security cameras throughout the building acting as his eyes and a dozen security officers as his ears, Reiniger knew how to press his advantage.

Blake would have nowhere to hide.

FORTY-FOUR

The trunk of Gerard's car was fully stocked. Leopold picked out a customized Taser unit that acted as both a flashlight and stunner. The device looked like a regular flashlight, but, according to the reference manual, packed enough punch to knock a two-hundred pound adult to the floor in less than a second. Leopold also selected a change of clothes from the suitcase that Gerard had provided; a dark blue suit, white shirt, and black loafers. With the trunk lid raised, he quickly changed and tossed his old outfit onto the back seat. Just in case he picked out one of the smaller knives that Gerard had hidden in the lining of the suitcase and slipped it into his inside pocket.

"You look very nice," said Mary. "But I'm not sure how that helps. You still look like you."

"I only need to get to the security office without setting off any alarms," said Leopold. "If I use the service entrance, there are fewer cameras. Once I disable the surveillance circuits, I should be able to blend in with the other office workers. So long as I keep away from the security guards, nobody should recognize me." He fastened his jacket button. "A well-tailored suit is the perfect camouflage in a place like this."

"And how do you plan on getting in?"

"Leave that to me. Just remember your part of the plan."

"We remember," said Sophie. "We just don't think it's going to work."

"That never stopped us before," said Mary. "How will we know when to make our move? You've got the only cell phone."

"Wait until I've killed the cameras. You'll see the little red lights go out. Then you move."

"No problem."

"Just one last thing." Leopold moved closer. "Be careful. If this works, the German will be coming for you. Don't try to confront him. Just run and hide. You understand?"

"Same goes for you," said Mary. "I reckon I can hold my own, but I'm not so sure about you." She jabbed him in the shoulder. It hurt more than Leopold expected.

"Okay, I get the point." He rubbed his arm. "Same goes for you, Sophie. Keep with Mary at all times. She knows what she's doing."

"I'm sure she does," said Sophie, looking the police sergeant up and down. "Just be careful."

Leopold slipped the Taser flashlight up his jacket sleeve and nodded. "Let's go."

Mary and Sophie walked off toward the main entrance, just around the corner from where were parked. Heading off in the opposite direction, Leopold aimed for the delivery yard, where he could see a handful of trucks parked up behind an iron gate. A security booth blocked the entrance, requiring all visitors without a key card to sign in.

With a curt wave, Leopold jogged up to the office door and knocked on the glass. The guard waved him inside. Glancing around, Leopold noticed there weren't any security cameras inside the tiny office. The guard was sat on a swivel chair behind a cramped desk.

"*Comment puis-je vous aider?*"

"*Bonjour,* I'm sorry, do you speak English?"

"Yes. How can I help?"

"I'm here to visit *Monsieur* Harris. Can you let me through?"

"Let me check the visitor log."

Leopold stepped forward. "Sorry about this, by the way."

The guard looked up. Leopold leaned across the desk, letting the Taser slip down into his hand. He held down the switch and jabbed the end into the man's neck. After a moment of convulsing, Leopold pulled away and the gatekeeper flopped onto his front, his face slapping hard against the wood.

Acting quickly, the consultant unhooked the guard's key card and removed his jacket. Slipping it over his own, Leopold zipped it up and fastened the key card to his belt. He dropped the Taser to the floor, its batteries depleted. Leopold took the back door and stepped out into the delivery yard, heading straight for the loading bay.

Ahead, past the dormant delivery trucks, stood a set of double doors. Leopold pushed through keeping his head down and prayed that nobody noticed his peculiar combination of puffer jacket and tailored trousers. The employees inside, many of whom were enjoying a late breakfast around the vending machines, paid him no notice as he slipped through the busy common room.

He found the door that led through to the service corridors and followed the signs toward the surveillance office. From his previous visits under less drastic circumstances, Leopold knew all the support facilities were housed on the ground floor, with the upper stories dedicated to office space and server storage. His target was just around the corner.

He passed a handful of people in the corridors, most of whom glanced at the 'Securitas' logo stitched into his jacket before looking away. Nobody stopped to speak to him. He avoided looking at the cameras. A few feet ahead, a locked door marked with the words "*Danger d'Électrocution*" and a yellow triangular sign showing a stick figure getting struck by lightning. Leopold swiped the security guard's key card over the magnetic reader and heard the lock click open.

Stepping through, Leopold found himself in a gloomy hallway and closed the door behind him. An untidy mass of multicolored wires ran in bunches along the wall, providing power to different areas of the building. He followed the cables through to a heavily air-conditioned room that was cold enough to make him shiver through both jackets. In the center of the room stood a wall of circuit breaker panels, mounted against a central support bracket. Each locked cabinet contained several dozen breakers, designed to shut down a particular circuit if it became overloaded.

Leopold pulled out Sophie's cell phone, bringing up the schematics he had downloaded earlier. He selected the set of breakers he needed and forced the lock open with the knife. Leopold used the light from the phone's screen to locate the circuits he'd have to disable – the ones that fed the security cameras. Simply flipping the switches wouldn't work, as they were designed to automatically realign after a few seconds. Instead, Leopold took the knife and severed the cables, permanently disrupting the power supply.

Slipping the knife back into his pocket, Leopold turned his attention back to the cell phone. He downloaded a copy of the photographs he had taken in the art gallery and sent them via picture message to the last incoming number in the phone's call history. Accompanying the photos, Leopold included the subject line: "Corner office. Top floor. 335962."

He waited for the message to go through and put the phone away. Tossing the guard's jacket in a trash can on his way out, Leopold headed for one of the stairwells that led to the upper floors.

FORTY-FIVE

The automatic doors slid open and Mary led Sophie through to the cavernous lobby. Inside, the air conditioning was on full blast and the receptionist looked as though she was trying not to shiver. Her desk sat in the middle of the floor, and she looked up as the two women approached.

Mary smiled politely and took a seat in the waiting area, thumbing through the magazines that had been left out. At the far end of the room she could see the elevators and a door leading through to the stairs. Glancing up, she could make out at least four security cameras, each with blinking red lights. She tapped her fingers against the chair.

"What's the plan?" asked Sophie.

"Keep an eye on those cameras," said Mary, pointing. "When the lights go out, that means the power's been cut. After that, we need to kick up a storm and divert the security guards down here while Leopold heads for the top floor."

"What about that man with the gun? If he's here, he'll come for us too."

"That's the intention, I'm afraid. Don't worry, I'll keep us safe."

Sophie didn't look convinced.

"Just stay close, okay?" said Mary. "Look," she pointed again. "The lights on the cameras have gone out. It's time to move."

The police sergeant got to her feet and walked over to the reception desk.

"You speak English?" she asked.

The receptionist nodded.

"Good. Now listen, I demand to speak to whoever the hell runs this place. I made some, erm" she glanced down at some of the corporate literature spread across the desk, "I made some big investments that didn't work out. I lost a lot of money. I need to speak with someone, now."

The receptionist sighed. "You have an account representative?" she asked, looking at Mary's crumpled clothes. "You need to speak to them about our policies on how we handle our clients' money. There is nothing I can do from here."

Mary slapped both palms down on the desk. "Hey, don't handle me. I lost a lot of money thanks to your company's incompetence. And not just me, either." She waved Sophie over. "Her too."

"*Madame*, please. I can't help you. Please arrange an appointment with your account executive. I'm sure he will be able to help both you and your daughter."

Sophie bit her lip and looked away.

Mary resisted the urge to slap the receptionist across the head. "We're not going anywhere, you understand?" She noticed some of the other people in the lobby start to pay attention. "Get the CEO down here, right now. It's about time you big corporations started taking some accountability for all the pain and misery you've caused."

"Yeah, we're not going anywhere," said Sophie, approximating an American accent. "And she's my sister."

"Make sure you get that last bit right," said Mary. "And don't go trying to palm us off on someone else. We demand to see the boss."

The receptionist rolled her eyes and lifted her telephone. "*Bonjour, oui, c'est moi. Envoyez sécurité maintenant, s'il vous plait. Merci.*" She hung up. "Security are on the way. Please leave."

Mary smiled. "Bring it on."

FORTY-SIX

The earbud crackled and Reiniger heard the orders come through. Two women were causing a scene in the lobby and the security cameras were malfunctioning. The assassin swore as he reached the ground floor. Blake had obviously created an diversion, but without surveillance to cover the rest of the building, Reiniger knew the cop and the girl were the only leads he had.

He would just have to persuade them to cooperate.

FORTY-SEVEN

Half a dozen uniformed guards strode across the lobby in Mary and Sophie's direction. A few paces behind them, the German was barking orders. He was still dressed in the charcoal suit, a slight bulge in his jacket giving away the handgun he wore holstered to his ribs. The guards began to fan out.

"Time to go," said Mary, grabbing hold of Sophie's wrist.

"Ow!"

"Just follow me."

The police sergeant dragged the younger woman away from the reception desk, heading toward a set of doors that led through to some of the lower offices. Mary noticed a suit approaching the entrance from behind the glass, reaching for his key card. They broke into a jog, catching hold of the door as he passed through.

"*Hé, toi!*"

"Keep moving!" Mary snatched the man's pass out of his hand as they barged past, slamming the door behind them.

Ahead, an open plan office stretched out to the edge of the building, broken up by a series of partitions. The room was crammed full of workers hunched over their desks, with others scurrying between meeting rooms carrying stacks of paper. Nobody looked up.

"Where now?" asked Sophie, out of breath.

Mary looked through the glass door panels and saw the guards approaching from fifty feet away. "We need to hide, to keep them focused on us for as long as possible. Leopold won't need long."

"What if they catch us?"

"Don't think about that." She started walking, keeping a fast pace, and aimed for the fire exits at the far wall. "If we can get onto the next floor, we might have better luck."

They pushed on, weaving between the desks. A few of the employees gave them puzzled looks, but nobody interfered. As they reached the halfway point, Mary heard raised voices and turned her head. The German and his team of guards had arrived.

"Keep going, nearly there," she said, speeding up. Allowing herself one more glance, she saw the German lock eyes with her from across the room. She quickly faced forward again. "Try not to look back. Through here."

They reached the far end of the office and Mary pushed through a heavy wooden fire door, leading to a set of concrete stairs. She looked up.

"These go all the way to the top. We need to keep the guards on the lower levels if we can."

"There should be plenty of meeting rooms to hide in," said Sophie.

"Let's hope so." Mary sucked in a deep breath before heading off, feeling her legs start to burn.

FORTY-EIGHT

Reiniger led the six guards across the office floor and through to the stairwell. He paused as they reached the steps.

"Sir, orders?" One of the uniforms asked.

"They couldn't have gone far," he said. "Split up. I'll take the second floor."

The security guards nodded and set off up the stairs, each headed for a different level. Reiniger followed, veering off at the top of the first flight. He pushed through the fire door and glanced around. Ahead, another identical office area opened up. In the middle was a bank of meeting rooms, surrounded on all sides by desks of varying sizes and shapes. The open-plan design seemed to encourage employees to get up and walk around, and Reiniger noticed that anyone not chained to a telephone was either chatting with a colleague or in the process of making themselves coffee. The noise and hustle was enough that it was unlikely anyone would notice two women pass through.

Reiniger made his way toward the meeting rooms in the center, glancing around as he walked. Human nature, he knew, would compel his targets to seek a hiding place rather than risk engaging him, but they could only stay hidden for so long. Reiniger only hoped he had the chance to find them before the others did.

Although the security guards were well paid and generally did as they were told, Reiniger doubted their stomachs could cope with what he had in mind. In his years as a contract assassin, the German had been given plenty of opportunity to hone his skills at extracting information from unwilling subjects, and he was keen to revisit some of his old practices. Though many of his contemporaries preferred the shock and awe effect of complicated torture equipment, Reiniger liked to keep it simple. Often, the tip of a knife blade was all that was needed to exact maximum pain. On many occasions just the threat of having one's skin peeled off was enough to ensure compliance. If more persuasion were needed, Reiniger had seen great success with removing a subject's fingernails. The pain was excruciating, but there was very little blood loss – meaning the interviewee almost never died as a result. Almost.

The assassin wasn't sure which method would be needed in this case. All he knew was that he looked forward to finding out.

FORTY-NINE

The meeting room was dark and empty, except for a conference table and ceiling-mounted projector. The walls were thin, probably made from the same material as the desk partitions, and there was practically zero soundproofing. All the noise from the printers and fax machines outside seeped through, along with the babble of a hundred different conversations going on. Though she was running for her life, Mary caught herself wondering who the hell still used fax machines.

"He'll find us in here," whispered Sophie.

Both women sat on the floor, away from the windows.

"Just keep quiet," said Mary. "This building has twenty stories, and each floor must have at least two dozen meeting rooms. By the time they check them all, Leopold will be done."

"Or they'll catch him too."

"Don't worry, they won't." Mary wasn't sure who she was trying to convince.

Sophie opened her mouth to say something, then changed her mind.

"What is it?"

"*Pardonnez-moi*, it's nothing. I mean, given the circumstances.. really, it's nothing."

Mary sat up a little. "No, go on. What is it? It's not like we've got anything else to talk about."

Sophie bit her lower lip. "It's just... I don't get what the deal is with him, you know?"

"What do you mean?"

"He's got all this money, a big company to run, all these responsibilities – and he spends his time playing Sherlock Holmes? I just don't get it."

"It's a little complicated."

"People keep saying that. I think I have the right to know."

Mary sighed. "You ever heard of Robert and Gisele Blake?"

"No. Are they related?"

"Yes, they were Leopold's parents. Very well known in their time, always in the papers for one thing or another."

"They died?"

"Yes. A mountaineering accident, but Leopold doesn't talk about it much. It took me years just to get that far with him. He never really accepted the fact they were gone, you know?"

"Why?"

"His mother's body was recovered, but they never found his father's. Leopold was convinced he was still out there somewhere. Even when the courts declared Robert Blake legally dead and Leopold inherited the company, he never gave up."

"His dad meant that much to him?"

Mary frowned. "No, it wasn't that. Not exactly. They way Leopold tells it, his father wasn't exactly a role

223

model. Though he never speaks about it, not directly anyway, it's possible his father was violent toward him and his mother. It's not something I tend to bring up in conversation, but I have my own theories."

"So why does he look for him?"

"I think he wants answers, to find the truth. Getting to the truth has always been an obsession, ever since I've known him. He's always felt like he needs to help other people find answers too. I guess it helps him come to terms with his own issues."

"He's a little crazy in the head, isn't he?" said Sophie.

"Oh undoubtedly. But not in the way you think. He's really quite brilliant, you know. Impulsive and reckless, but also brilliant."

"How did you meet?"

"It was only a few years after the mountaineering accident. Leopold was a complete wreck at the time, dosed up on God-knows-what, and trying to track down someone who was apparently trying to blackmail him. Let's just say he's come a long way since then."

"What happened?"

Mary hesitated. "First time I met him, I arrested him for assault and being under the influence of illegal drugs. Once he sobered up, he explained what was going on. I said I'd help him if he agreed to clean up his act. He agreed, and actually proved to be useful in catching the blackmailer. The rest is history."

"And I guess he never found out what happened to his father?"

"That's the funny thing – whenever I ask him about it, he shuts down. It's like he's hiding something from me."

"I guess he has a lot of secrets," said Sophie.

"More than we'll ever know."

"And what happens if Leopold can't get what he needs from Harris?"

"The police have enough evidence to put all three of us in prison. And from what I've seen today, I don't think any of us would last very long in there – I doubt we'd even make it to a trial. If Leopold can't get something on Harris, we're screwed. And that's if the psychotic German doesn't catch up with us first."

"You have faith in him, don't you?"

"In the German? I've got faith he'll torture us to death if he gets to us before the police do." She noticed Sophie recoil. "Oh, you meant Leopold."

"*Oui*, I can tell you think highly of him."

Mary smiled. "He takes a bit of getting used to."

"You don't see the way he looks at you, do you?"

"What, me? Don't be stupid."

"And you always smile a little when you talk about him."

Mary put a hand to her mouth. "Let's just change the subject."

"Okay, so this German guy," said Sophie, obliging. "He's going to torture us to death?"

"Don't worry, he's not going to find –" She froze. The unmistakable sound of scuffling feet coming from outside. "Keep down," she said, turning to Sophie. "Someone's coming."

A shadow crossed the window.

"Get ready to run. When I say…"

The door handle moved.

"One… Two…"

The door opened.

"Three!"

FIFTY

Rousseau circled the Dubois residence for the fifth time, in the process of deciding whether or not to chase down the tech who had promised him quick results. Just as he made up his mind, his cell phone buzzed. Before he could pull over to read the message, the car's hands-free system registered an incoming call and the speakers started blasting out a shrill ringtone. Rousseau grimaced and answered.

"*Capitaine*, this is Jean-Pierre." It was the tech from earlier. "I've successfully cloned the cell phone you gave me and sent the original down to evidence. I'm forwarding all incoming text messages and calls to you. It looks like you might have something already. Do the numbers '335962' mean anything to you?"

"*Non,* not that I can think of. Do you have a trace on the owner?"

"The cell phone is registered to an American. I pulled some strings at the embassy and had them run the records – it belongs to a cop with the NYPD. Her name is Mary Jordan. The last call is from one of the suspects, Sophie Bardot."

"A cop is mixed up in all this?"

"Looks that way."

"Can you get a location?"

"*Oui*, I pinged Mlle. Bardot's handset. We've narrowed it down to a cell tower near La Defense. The techs are working to get ."

"Good. Send the address to my GPS system when you have it. I'll make my way there now. Arrange for a backup team to join me once you have the location."

"Yes, sir. We should have it within five minutes."

"I'll be halfway there by then. Make sure you hurry."

Rousseau hung up and activated the police cherry still fixed to his roof, turning the car toward the main road that led out to the Boulevard Périphérique – the highway that would take him straight to La Defense. The other cars moved to let him pass and Rousseau floored it.

He hit the open road at speed, and shifted into a fast cruise. Despite the breakthrough with the cell phone, something didn't feel right. Who was the gunman who brought down his men in the parking lot? How did an American cop get involved? Why was she receiving phone calls from one of the other suspects, one she was travelling with? And, above all, how could a trained professional be careless enough to leave a cell phone where Rousseau could easily find it?

This whole case stank, and Blake owed him answers. Even if Rousseau had to lock the arrogant bastard up for twenty years to get them.

FIFTY-ONE

Leopold strode through the upper offices, having climbed nearly nineteen flights of stairs, and tried not to pass out. He knew better than to use the elevators with most of the building's security looking for him, but the long climb had sapped most of the strength out of his legs and his head was spinning. If anyone caught up with him now, he'd have no chance of getting away.

With sweat starting to show through the front of his shirt, Leopold pulled his jacket tighter to hide the stains. With his head down, he made a bee line for the elevator, the only way up to Harris' office on the twentieth floor.

He grabbed a stack of important-looking papers from an empty desk and kept moving, hoping to pass for one of the associates. Nearly bumping into half a dozen people on his way through, he eventually reached the elevator and dumped the pile of reports into a trash can. He hoped he hadn't just got someone fired.

Leopold jabbed the call button and stepped inside as the doors slid open. He used the buttons to punch in the code "335962." The doors closed and the elevator shuddered to life, heading upward. Leopold took a deep breath and willed his muscles to stop aching. He was going to need them.

FIFTY-TWO

The blinds were down, the lights were off, and all the other meeting rooms were in use. Reiniger strode over, listening out for any movement inside. He turned the handle, slowly at first, reaching inside his jacket for his gun. Finger on the trigger, he kicked out with his foot. The door flew open.

"What the hell, buddy?" the man spoke English, an American accent.

The assassin froze. A conference table in the center of the room seated six people, each staring dumbfounded in Reiniger's direction. On the far wall, a projected image of some sales figures. A few pie charts.

"What do you want?" the man asked again. His tone had shifted from surprised to pissed off.

Reiniger straightened, taking his hand out of his jacket. "My apologies, wrong meeting room." He turned and walked out. As he closed the door behind him, he felt his cell phone buzz with an incoming message:

"Blake used his pass code. On his way up. Come now."

Reiniger frowned. He had hoped to catch up with the two women first, maybe get some alone time with them. They owed him for all the trouble he'd gone through in the last twenty-four hours.

Still, things could be worse.

Just as Harris predicted, Blake had acted like a reckless fool. By forcing a confrontation, he had put his life, and the lives of others, at risk. Having escaped twice already, a sensible man would have cut his losses and made a run for it. Instead, Blake was walking right into a trap. And for what?

The assassin headed for the elevators, keen to ask Blake for an answer in person.

FIFTY-THREE

The elevator doors slid open at the twentieth floor, reserved for the company's top brass. Ahead, Leopold could see Harris' corner office, backed up against the tall windows that looked out at the midmorning city skyline. The door was closed and the blinds were drawn. Between Leopold and the office, several dozen executives and interns busied themselves with paperwork and morning coffee runs.

He stepped out onto the carpet, looking around. Leopold had visited the Paris office several times over the last few years, and his face was well known to the more senior executives. Several employees glanced up as he walked past, conversations halted mid-sentence, and some even reached for their cell phones – presumably to call security. Or maybe the police.

It didn't matter now. Leopold knew this was his last chance to make a stand and, whatever the outcome, it was better than the prospect of spending the rest of his life on the run. He drew closer to the office door. A small crowd was starting to form around him now, and the consultant felt fifty pairs of eyes following his movements.

His heart starting to pound, Leopold took out the cell phone he borrowed from Sophie and hit redial. He dropped the handset back into his pocket as he reached Harris' door, praying everything went to plan.

FIFTY-FOUR

The squints over at forensics sent the cell phone's location through within five minutes, better than promised. Rousseau was following the route set by his smart phone's satellite navigation software and was getting close when the handset started to ring. The *capitaine* nearly slammed on the brakes when he realized who was calling. He patched the call through to the car's speakers.

Something on the other end of the line he couldn't make out. Was that static? Rousseau hit the 'record' button and concentrated on the road ahead. The Blake Investments building loomed ahead, a column of polished glass among a dozen other identical structures. Backup was on the way, a few minutes behind. He would need to find somewhere to wait for them. A sound from the speakers grabbed his attention. Voices. Muffled, but unmistakable. He could just about make out what they were saying.

Rousseau swore and dropped a gear, revving the car's engine to the redline.

FIFTY-FIVE

"You here to kill me, Blake?"

Leopold stood in the doorway. Harris stood behind his desk, his back to the tall windows. The sun was behind him, an old trick. Leopold had hoped to open the conversation differently, but anything that got Rousseau there quicker was okay with him.

"And why would I want to kill you?" he said.

Leopold knew Harris well. For nearly a decade, he had entrusted the smooth running of the European Divisions to the man. Trust that had been horribly misplaced. But Harris was no fool, and certainly smart enough not to get drawn into a trap. Leopold would just have to be smarter.

"I understand this is a difficult time," said Harris. "Just so you know, the board and I will give you our full support. We know these things the police are saying…" he paused. "Well, we'll be sure to help you through this." A smile.

"Thank you for your concern. But I'm not here to talk about that."

"Oh?"

"The bodyguard you sent. Gerard. I'm sorry to say he didn't make it."

Harris raised an eyebrow.

"His blood is on your hands. Along with Dubois'. And the four other people at the cathedral."

"I have no idea what you're talking about, Blake."

"And if you let the sale of Chemworks go through, there will be even more blood. Maybe even yours."

"Are you threatening me?"

"I'm just outlining your situation."

"Which is?"

Leopold took a step forward. "Best case scenario for you: the police figure out what you've been up to and have you arrested. You spend the rest of your natural life in prison."

"Oh, I see. And, just out of curiosity, what's the worst case scenario in this little fantasy of yours?"

"The police *don't* arrest you and the very, very bad people you've gotten yourself involved with decide they have too many loose ends."

Harris chuckled. "You sound like you have some experience with these people yourself, Leopold."

"I do. Enough experience to know there's someone else calling the shots. You have the stink of a powerless man, Harris."

Leopold felt something cold and hard press into the back of his skull. He saw Harris smile.

"What was that you were saying about powerless, Blake?" a voice came from behind. Deep, with a German accent.

"Yes, I think you'll find *I'm* calling the shots after all," said Harris. He moved out from behind his desk and walked toward Leopold. Leaning forward, he reached into the consultant's jacket and pulled out the cell phone. He dropped it to the floor.

"Is that the same gun you used to kill Gerard?" said Leopold.

"Don't say a word," said Harris, before the German could reply. He turned his attention back to the cell phone, now lying on the carpet. "This is just in case."

Harris stamped his foot down onto the phone. He continued until it shattered into three separate pieces.

FIFTY-SIX

Rousseau heard the phone line go dead. The Blake Investments building was the next right, and the captain didn't even slow down to take the corner. The Renault sedan drifted, sliding over the asphalt at forty miles per hour before hitting the parking lot. By the time he slammed on the brakes, Rousseau had filled the cabin with the stink of burnt rubber.

The entrance lobby was fifty feet away. Rousseau switched off the ignition and jumped out of the car, leaving the vehicle parked haphazardly across two empty spaces. He broke into a sprint, aging bones crying out in protest. Reaching the automatic doors, Rousseau paused to let them slide open and felt his heart pounding in his chest.

Whatever Blake was doing, he was going to get himself killed.

The glass doors opened and the captain resumed running, ignoring the protests of the woman at the reception desk. A few people milling around the foyer looked over at him as he ran past, heading for the elevators. He jabbed the call button and stepped inside as the car arrived.

Double checking the photo message he had received earlier, Rousseau punched in the numbers '335962' and felt the elevator start to move. He dialed dispatch.

"*Oui, vous-aider?*" The same bored desk jockey as before.

"This is Rousseau. I'm on scene at the Blake Investments Building. Where the hell is my backup?"

A short pause on the line. "I have the details, sir. Your backup team is en route. Five minutes."

"I don't have time to wait. Get a message to the unit leader and tell him to seal off the building. I'll also need a team up on the top floor."

No answer.

"Got that?"

"Yes, sir."

"Then why are you still on the Goddamn line?" Rousseau hung up and took in a deep breath. Although he didn't consider himself out of shape, he made a mental promise to start exercising more often. Maybe even try a diet.

He hit the seventh floor and felt the car start to slow. On the eighth floor, the elevator stopped and the doors slid open. Four suits stood waiting in the hallway, each carrying a folder stuffed with papers. They stepped forward.

"*Je suis désolé,*" said Rousseau, opening his jacket to reveal his sidearm and badge. "*Occupé.*" He hit the button to close the doors and smiled as the suits disappeared from view.

The elevator set off again and Rousseau composed himself. He had heard two other voices on the phone earlier in addition to Blake's, one with an American accent and one that sounded German. Blake had mentioned a gun. Something about the German gave Rousseau shivers, a feeling that he couldn't shake off. Probably just the effects of the adrenaline pumping through his blood. The captain put one hand on his service revolver.

Twelfth floor.

The low rumble of the elevator reached a crescendo. The walls of the car seemed a little closer in than before.

Fifteenth floor.

The captain steadied his breathing and ran through a mental checklist: Backup was on the way. There were six rounds in the barrel of his revolver and extra rounds in his pocket, just in case.

Eighteenth floor.

He wasn't wearing a protective vest.

His hand was shaking a little.

He wasn't as good a marksman as he used to be.

He wasn't exactly getting any younger, either.

His muscles ached.

Rousseau told himself to stop worrying. Thirty years on the force was long enough to develop an instinct. Muscle memory and gut reactions had kept him alive so far, and he wasn't about to break the habit.

Nineteenth floor.

Nearly there. Rousseau kept his hand on his gun and watched the elevator lights announce the next stop.

Twentieth floor.

A soft chiming noise announced his arrival. The doors opened.

Time to move.

FIFTY-SEVEN

Leopold heard the crunch of glass under Harris' shoe. The cell phone was destroyed, completely useless. The police wouldn't even be able to track it. Hopefully, Rousseau had taken the bait already.

"We won't be needing that, I think." Harris reached forward and took the gun away from the German. "It doesn't really look too good, does it? A gunshot wound to the back of the head doesn't really scream 'self-defense'. We'll have to be a little rough around the edges this time, Reiniger."

Harris lay the gun on the desk and walked around to his chair. Leopold heard a drawer open.

"When a wanted murderer breaks into your office and attacks you, it's far more likely you'll end up in a bit of a struggle." Harris pulled out a heavy-looking revolver and lay it down next to the German's pistol. "I reckon it's more likely an intruder would get hit in the chest. What do you think, Reiniger?"

Leopold turned his head and saw the German nod. It was definitely the same man from Dubois' house, still dressed in the suit he was wearing when he murdered Gerard. The man's expression was cold, impassive.

There was a spark of something ruthless in his eyes. Leopold knew the look well.

"Good," Harris continued. "Why don't you give me and Mr. Blake a little time alone? We've got some catching up to do. Keep an eye out for any other visitors."

Reiniger turned and left the room without another word.

"So, this is what it all comes down to," said Leopold. "All this, just for a chunk of money? You'd betray everything we built together?"

Harris picked up the revolver, weighing it in both hands. "Everything *you* built. Everything your *father* built. I was along for the ride, sure. At first, that was all I needed. But after ten years, fifteen years, hell…" he smiled. "After *twenty* years working with you and your father, what do I have to show for it? You don't pay that well, you know. And the way you're going about running this place, the whole company is going to be looking at bankruptcy in a few years. I've got to start thinking about retirement, Leopold. After a lifetime of working my ass off, I deserve the chance to live a little, don't you think?"

"Business is booming, Harris," said Leopold. "You got greedy, that's all."

"You really have no idea, do you?" He shook his head and stepped out from behind the desk. "We're struggling to break even. And that's on a good year. If you spent more time in the office, where you belong, and less time playing cops and robbers, you'd know that. But so long as your trust fund stays topped up, you really don't care, do you? The sale of Chemworks is the only thing that can really get us back in the game. And I knew you'd be too blind to go along with it."

"And that's why you kept things from me, all these years," said Leopold. "This was your intention the whole time."

"Not the whole time," said Harris. "But when we made the discovery… Well, suffice it to say my eyes were open to what was possible with the right attitude and approach." He shook his head. "The Chemworks business is a regulatory nightmare. If anyone found out what we were doing," he paused. "Still, none of that matters now. With you out of the picture, I can take control of your shares and push the sale through with the other stockholders. The board will sign off the paperwork and it's a done deal. We get an injection of capital to get us through another few years, and I get a significant boost in my investment portfolio – enough to make sure I never have to work another day in my life. It's a win-win situation. It's a shame you won't be around to enjoy it."

"Don't do this, Harris. You have no idea what these buyers will do with the company. If that sort of research fell into the wrong hands, the results could be devastating."

"Relax. You're being paranoid."

"I suppose you did your due diligence, did you? Or was the lure of the money too tempting to question their motives?"

Harris shook his head. "Why should I care? I spent my whole life doing what other people thought was the right thing. Now it's my turn."

"People have died. Can't you see what's happening here?"

"People like Dubois? His own greed was his downfall. Do you know how easy it was to convince him to arrange the break-in? Once I found out the Louvre was kicking him to the curb, it was a done deal."

"But why?"

"You can work it out, I'm sure." Harris leaned against the desk, holding the gun loosely by his side. "You're supposed to be the smart one, after all."

"It was all about me, wasn't it?"

"There's that ego again." Harris rolled his eyes.

"You needed me in Paris for this to work, and you knew I'd never turn down a job with the Louvre. But you had to give them a strong enough reason to hire me."

"A stolen painting seemed like a strong enough reason. After the FBI Director recommended you, it was in the bag. Or, at least, someone who sounded a lot like the FBI Director on the phone."

"And once you had me in place, all you had to do was have your Rottweiler set me up and make sure everything went down smoothly." He shook his head. "What I still don't understand is why you killed all those people at the cathedral. They were no threat to you. Why did they have to die?"

"No loose ends, like you said. And with you in prison, without that bodyguard of yours to keep an eye on you, it was inevitable that something bad was going to happen eventually. I expect your giant friend is learning that for himself."

"Those people died for no reason," said Leopold. "There were never any loose ends. You killed innocent people just to make me look like more of a killer. You didn't need to do that."

"Oh, but I did. But you'll never know why." He raised the gun. "It's enough for me to know that I beat you. That I'm smarter than you."

Leopold sighed. "You went to a lot of trouble. And for what? I'm still here. A smart man would have just killed me in the first place."

Harris smiled and took a step forward, aiming the revolver at Leopold's chest. "There's still time for that."

FIFTY-EIGHT

Rousseau strode toward the corner office on the top floor, his open jacket revealing his badge and gun. He ignored the anxious looks and focused on his target. From fifty feet away, he could make out silhouettes against the blinds. There were people in there. Two people. But Rousseau had heard three voices on the phone before the line had gone dead – so where was the other?

He didn't have to wait long for an answer. Rousseau felt movement before he saw it, something approaching from behind at speed. The captain turned and registered a gray blur, moving too fast to follow. Then the pain came.

Rousseau felt his head snap to the side. He fell to the floor and rolled, instinctively reaching for his gun as he got up to his knees. He looked up for his target and saw a man dressed in a charcoal suit. His face was familiar. Pain hit again as the captain brought his revolver around and the suit kicked out, knocking the weapon from his hand on to the floor.

That's when everyone started to panic. Someone must have seen the gun and started screaming. There was a stampede as the office workers realized what was going on and decided to make a run for it. Most of them headed for the elevator, while the smarter ones either dashed for the stairwell or ducked under their desks. A few ran close by, scrambling for the exits, separating the captain from his attacker.

The respite was welcome. Rousseau got to his feet and let his training take over. He recognized the man's face now, from the parking lot camera footage. Wearing a suit this time, but unmistakable. The tall, broad shoulders and ruthless face, the obvious muscle around the arms and neck. Was this the man with the German accent on the phone? Rousseau shook the questions out of his head, gritted his teeth, and charged.

The *capitaine* lowered his shoulder and went for the knees. The suit tried to move, but Rousseau was too fast. He lifted the German off the floor and didn't stop driving forward until he hit one of the partition walls. The whole thing shook from the impact, but the suit didn't make a sound. Rousseau felt a jolt of pain in his shoulder and lost his grip. He saw the German's knee come up and felt his nose crunch. Something wet dripping down his face. A white-hot daze of pain and disorientation filled him.

Stumbling backward, Rousseau tried to put some distance between them. The suit moved fast, covering the floor in two steps. Something in his hand. Was that a knife? The pain came again as the German lashed out and Rousseau danced to the side, but too late. He glanced at his arm and saw the tear – a deep red gash beneath his jacket sleeve.

The office workers finally worked out the elevators weren't going to work out for such a large crowd and turned back, heading for the stairs. They froze as they realized Rousseau and his opponent were in the way. At least three dozen people stood staring, dumbfounded. Then someone saw Rousseau's badge.

"Look! The Police!" A chubby man with a goatee pointed.

"He's hurt," said someone else, out of sight.

The German held up the knife. Rousseau noticed his police service revolver, maybe ten feet away, lying on the floor. Within reach of the crowd.

"There's a gun," one of the workers said.

"Don't touch it!" said another.

"But we can help."

"You don't know how to shoot." Another voice joined in.

"I know better than you."

"How the hell would you know?"

The bickering continued. Rousseau looked over at the German, a little more than an arm's length away. The captain could see every muscle in the man's body tensed, ready to strike. Rousseau knew he didn't stand a chance against his younger, stronger opponent – but, luckily, he had something the German didn't.

"This is your last chance to walk away from this," Rousseau said, looking into his attacker's eyes with as much bravado as he could muster.

"I think you may have misread the situation," the German replied. "You are wounded and without a weapon."

"For now. But what happens when that crowd figure out they can pick up the gun and use it. I'm the only one with one of these." He tapped his badge. "Who do you think they'll aim for?"

The German paused.

"Make the smart move and get out of here. My men aren't looking for you. There'll be nobody to get in the way. If you stay, this won't end well for you."

The German appeared to consider the offer, keeping one eye on the rabble of office workers.

"What's in this for you anymore?" Rousseau continued. "Whatever plans you had involving Blake are over. Killing me won't make any difference, except to put you in the sights of every single cop in Paris. In *France*." He kept eye contact, his pulse racing in his ears. "Do you really want that?"

The German lowered the knife.

"I didn't think so."

"You know what will happen if you try to come after me."

Rousseau nodded, watching his opponent turn and walk away. Without looking back, the German took the fire exit to the stairs and disappeared from view. He would have no trouble avoiding the backup teams – Rousseau knew they would be too busy looking for Blake and his accomplices.

The captain allowed himself a moment to catch his breath and picked up his firearm. The crowd fell silent, looking as though they expected him to take charge. As his fingers touched the grip, the sound of gunfire ripped through the room and he hit the floor, clutching at his head.

FIFTY-NINE

The pain was unreal. Leopold had been shot before, but it had never felt like this. Not even close. The round hit home like a sledgehammer, like running into a brick wall at fifty miles per hour. Nothing at first, then the nerve endings caught up and unleashed hell. His brain screamed with electric fury, but he kept his mouth clamped shut.

"Hurts, doesn't it?" said Harris, lowering the revolver. The barrel was smoking in a way that Leopold thought only ever happened in the movies. "Try to relax. This will all be over soon. I just had to make it look a little more... *realistic* first."

Leopold fought to see through the tears and noticed Harris pick up the German's pistol. He tossed the weapon at floor where Leopold was kneeling.

"I'm really not much of a marksman," said Harris. "You came at me with a gun and I panicked. Hit you in the shoulder before putting you down for good." He looked down at the gun. "Pick it up. Or I'll shoot you in the other shoulder."

Leopold complied, using his good arm. The pain was still too intense to come up with an alternative.

"Good. And before you get any bright ideas, I haven't loaded it yet. I want you to look me in the eyes; I want you to fully understand everything that's happening to you, and I want you to know that there's absolutely nothing you can do about it. It's a lesson you should have learned years ago." He pulled back the hammer.

The pain in Leopold's shoulder peaked. His whole upper arm felt as though it was going to fall off, but he could feel his other senses start to return after the initial shock of the impact. It was painful, but bearable. He looked up at Harris.

"Something to say, Blake? Better make it quick."

Leopold managed a weak smile. "There's just one thing," he said. "Can you hear that noise?"

Harris aimed the gun at Leopold's forehead. "What noise?"

"When I got here, the entire floor was packed full of people. The sound of printers and telephones, of people walking about. People having conversations."

"What are you talking about?"

"A couple of minutes ago it went quiet. Unfortunately, I think you were a little busy concentrating on your evil genius speech at the time. I'm glad I remembered to ask all the right questions." Leopold smiled. "Bad guys always love to talk. It's great when you need a little extra time."

"Get to the point, Blake." He spoke through his teeth.

"What would cause an entire floor full of people to fall silent? Either they've all gone home early, or someone else shut them up. Which do you think is more likely?"

Harris didn't reply.

Leopold winced as he shifted his weight. His legs had gone numb from kneeling on the floor. "Do you know how effective police scanning and tracking technologies are these days?" he continued. "They can pinpoint the location of any wireless radio device to within a few feet. A device like that, for example." He nodded at the broken remains of Sophie's cell phone. "Now, I'll ask again: just who do you suppose would cause an entire floor full of people to go completely quiet?"

Harris twitched.

"I'll give you a clue: it's probably not the janitor." Leopold sucked in a deep breath as a wave of pain hit him again. He wasn't sure how much longer he could keep this up. "Which is probably bad news for you."

"These are your last words Blake, I suggest you use them well."

"There are people looking for me, Harris. They know where I am. They know you're here with me. There might be someone on the other side of that door right now, waiting for his moment to burst in. If you kill me, the chances of you walking out of this building alive drop to zero. Do the smart thing. Walk away."

Stepping forward, Harris pressed the barrel of the gun against Leopold's forehead and smiled. "Nice try," he said. "It's a pity you'll never know how this worked out. Maybe in another life we could have been partners in this." He paused. "Goodbye, Mr. Blake."

Leopold saw Harris squeeze the trigger.

He closed his eyes.

The sound of the gunshot was overwhelming; it ripped through his eardrums and rattled inside his skull, flaring up the pain he had tried to push to the back of his mind. As the initial shock subsided and his higher senses returned, Leopold wondered how he had managed to hear the shot at all – he should have been dead before his brain had even processed the sound.

He opened his eyes slowly. There was Harris, standing as before with the revolver held in one hand, aimed directly at Leopold's head. There was a look of surprise on his face, a mix of shock and disbelief. His eyes were rolled upward, as though trying to focus on something in the air above him.

Then Leopold saw it. In the center of Harris' forehead, a small red dot. It was dripping with something. Leopold blinked and tried to focus. A quiet gurgle escaped from Harris' mouth and then he toppled backward, falling stiff and upright like a felled tree. He hit the floor hard and didn't make another sound. There was movement behind him.

"Looks like this is the end of the road for you, *Monsieur* Blake." A rough voice said with a heavy French accent.

Leopold turned his head and saw a figure in the doorway, holding something in front of him in both hands. The consultant couldn't quite make it out. His vision started to fade, rings of red and black forming in front of his eyes.

"You're bleeding badly," said the voice. "Can you stand?"

The words echoed and melded together. Leopold felt the world spin and the pain in his shoulder fade away. He felt his body hit the floor in slow motion. Just before he lost consciousness, he saw the figure in the doorway walk toward him.

Then darkness.

SIXTY

Leopold could hear the low hum of the air conditioning systems and it took a moment for him to realize where he was. There was something tugging at the skin at the crease of his elbow. He was lying on something soft. Leopold opened his eyes and winced as a bright light hit his pupils. He turned his head to look at his injured shoulder and found it cleaned and bandaged. There was a familiar hospital smell.

"Welcome back to the real world, *Monsieur* Blake," said a voice he recognized.

Leopold blinked and looked around. The privacy curtain twitched and *Capitaine* Rousseau of the Paris police stepped through. He stood next to Leopold's bed and looked down with a passive expression.

"You lost quite a lot of blood, I'm afraid," the captain said. "The doctors performed a transfusion and put you on a saline drip. You've been asleep for the last eight hours."

Leopold sat up and found that both his wrists had been handcuffed to the bed rails. His mouth was dry and scratchy.

"You might find it hard to move around with those on," said Rousseau. "They said you might feel a little nauseous. Here, drink this." The captain held a paper cup of water up to his lips.

Gulping down the cold liquid, Leopold felt a little energy return. "Where's Mary?"

"She's fine. Mlle. Bardot as well."

"I need to speak to them."

"I'm afraid the only person you'll be speaking to will be your lawyer."

"You've got to be kidding me. What about Harris?"

"I saw him, and I stopped him. But you still have a lot to answer for. And I never got the chance to read you your rights before you passed out."

"This is ridiculous. I want to –"

"You have the right to remain silent. You have the right to an attorney. You have… wait, that's not it." Rousseau scratched his chin. "Let me start again. You have the right to stay in bed… no, that's not it, either."

"Maybe I can help." Another familiar voice from behind the curtain.

Leopold saw the material twitch again and Mary swept through, a giant grin plastered on her face. Jerome followed behind, his burly frame blocking out most of the light. Mary laughed as she stepped up next to Rousseau.

"I'm sorry, I just really had to see your face," she said, still grinning from ear to ear. "Once we caught up with super-cop here, I showed him all the things we found on the safe house computer and at Dubois' place."

Jerome nodded. "We also got that report through on the victims from the Notre Dame shooting and some very interesting testimony from the prison warden. We're all in the clear; no charges are being brought."

255

"They should have just left you in prison," said Leopold.

"*Je suis désolé*, I'm sorry – but it was too tempting to resist," said Rousseau, also smiling. "We have enough evidence to pin this on Harris. There was another man too, a German, who we weren't able to find. We have Interpol running a search for suspects matching his description."

"What do you know about him?"

Rousseau scratched his stubble. "Not a lot. I imagine he changes identity and appearance for each job that he takes. And when I say 'job,' I think you know what I mean."

"From the look of his victims, I'd say the man has some serious skills," said Jerome. "I'd like to have the opportunity to meet him some day." He turned to Rousseau. "And when I say 'meet,' I think you know what I mean."

"The NYPD will help in any way we can," said Mary. "I'm sure Leopold will have a word with the FBI."

"Speaking of victims," said Leopold. "What came back in the report?"

Mary looked at Rousseau. "The young woman, the lawyer. She was hired by Blake Investments to handle the corporate handover after you were forced to step away from the research company," she said.

"Harris apparently paid her to change a few of the clauses in the contracts. It effectively gave him full control if anything ever happened to you," said Jerome.

"We ran her bank accounts," said Rousseau. "A single payment of forty thousand Euros was made to her around the time of the transfer. We also found a deposit from the same account listed against Jean

Dubois' recent transactions. Over a hundred thousand Euros."

"And what about the other victims? The other three people?" asked Leopold.

"Camouflage," said the captain. "To keep us from discovering the connection. If you hadn't been looking at this with your lives on the line... well, we probably wouldn't have caught it ourselves."

"Let's just be grateful my contact dug a little deeper." Leopold tugged on his handcuffs. "How about getting me out of these? We've got to stop the sale of Chemworks before the transfer papers go through. I don't know what kind of buyers Harris had lined up, but I'll bet he didn't worry too much about vetting them."

Mary and Rousseau looked at each other.

"What is it?"

"I'm afraid it's too late for that," said Rousseau. "The sale of Chemworks went through while you were unconscious. The contracts were ironclad; even if you had been there, you wouldn't have been able to stop it." He shrugged. "On the plus side, you seem to have been paid a very good price for your shares."

Leopold felt his stomach clench. "Who bought it?"

Mary folded her arms. "A company called INGX, whatever the hell that stands for. It's a shell corporation, what looks like a business structure set up to funnel cash away from the tax authorities. We can trace the parent company or subsidiary, but INGX is registered in Switzerland, so we have no jurisdiction. It might take some time."

"I'll send the details to the usual guy to check out," said Jerome. "He should be able to trace the parent company a little faster than the NYPD or Interpol." He looked at the two cops. "No offense."

"That's not exactly an encouraging sign," said Leopold. "Any company that goes to those lengths to protect its identity isn't exactly going to be Charity of the Year, is it? If Harris was telling the truth about the results Chemworks was seeing..." he trailed off.

Mary frowned and took out her cell phone. "Thanks for getting this back to me, Captain," she said, tapping the screen. "I'm afraid you'll have to excuse me. I think I need to make a phone call. It looks like I might owe someone an apology." She turned and walked out of the room.

"Her sister," said Leopold, in response to a quizzical look from Rousseau. "Works for the WHO. Apparently, they've been keeping an eye on Chemworks for a few years now. Definitely not my biggest fan, that one."

Jerome smiled. "You can't blame her for that."

"Well, gentlemen," said Rousseau. "This is my cue to leave, I think. I have a stack of paperwork waiting for me and a family to look after. If you decide to stay in Paris a few more days. Please try not to get into any more trouble."

Leopold and Jerome looked at each other. Neither replied.

"I thought as much. Just try to keep away from my side of town, *d'accord?* Okay?" Rousseau tipped an imaginary cap and sauntered out of the room, mumbling something to himself as he went.

"Where's Sophie?" asked Leopold.

"Outside, getting something to eat," said Jerome. "She said there was just one more thing she wanted to show us. Seemed pretty excited about it."

"We should probably get going then. I assume I'm fit to be discharged?"

"Sure. Just a little scratch, that's all. I don't know why you always make such a habit of passing out."

"Pardon me. I didn't realize I'd become so predictable," said Leopold.

"Maybe we can work on it for next time."

"There's going to be a next time?"

"Of course. I don't think this story's over quite yet. Now, are you coming or not?"

Leopold sighed. "I'd love to. There's just one thing." He tugged at his handcuffs again. "I might need a little help with these."

SIXTY-ONE

The sun was going down. Fat and pink, it sank slowly over the horizon and cast the city skyline in sharp relief against the white clouds gathering overhead. On the second level of the Eiffel Tower, four hundred feet above the ground, Leopold looked out over Paris as the evening chill began to set in. The wind picked up, whipping about his head, and he pulled his jacket around him a little tighter.

"What do you think?" a soft voice asked.

Sophie appeared from behind the corner and took Leopold's arm.

"It's quite extraordinary," said Leopold.

"Sorry it's a little cold. You get the best view on this level, even better than the viewing platform at the top. But you have to be outside."

Leopold nodded, wishing he'd brought a coat. "Thanks for showing it to me."

Sophie smiled. "We're not here just for you." She waved at Mary and Jerome, who were trying to find a coffee stand that was still serving. They made their way over, weaving through the sparse crowd of tourists who still remained.

"What do I have to do to get an espresso around here?" asked Mary, shivering. "It's freezing cold and I'm seriously jonesing for a caffeine fix. And I don't think I've tried so much as a croissant since I got here."

"I keep telling her you can't get a decent cup of coffee in Paris," said Jerome. "I think she's determined to prove me wrong."

"Whatever. I just need to eat, that's all."

"Relax, relax," said Sophie. "It's a beautiful evening and there are a hundred restaurants nearby that serve the best food you have ever tasted. For now, why not just enjoy the moment, just get lost in it. Come here," she let go of Leopold's arm and waved Mary over. "Just look out at the city. I promise you'll feel better."

Mary did as suggested and took a spot next to Leopold, up against the railings.

Sophie looked up at Jerome. "Maybe you and I should go find somewhere we can get a hot drink?"

"I think that's probably a good idea," he replied with the slightest trace of a grin.

The two of them walked off toward the elevators.

"What do you think that was all about?" said Mary, putting both hands on the iron rails. She let out a deep sigh and looked out over the horizon. "Wow, this place really is amazing."

Leopold felt his ears start to get hot, despite the chilly wind. "Yeah, I guess it is. I suppose when you've been used to seeing something like this for so long," he gestured at the sunset, "you start taking it for granted. Sometimes you need someone to remind you what's right in front of you." He looked at her. "You know what I mean?"

She smiled and looked back. "You know, until today I probably would have thought you were getting sentimental on me, Leopold. But now, I have to admit I'm inclined to agree." She tilted her head. "Penny for your thoughts?"

"Am I that obvious?"

"We've known each other a long time. I can read you like a book."

"I'll have to be more careful."

Mary turned her body to face him. "It's not a bad thing, Leopold. It means we're good partners. What's on your mind?"

"We're partners now are we?"

"Just answer the question, smartass."

He grinned, not feeling the cold quite so much any more. "With everything that's happened since you met me, all the close calls and near misses, do you think there will ever be an end to it all?"

"Like, do I think you'll ever learn to settle down?" She punched him playfully on the arm. "That doesn't sound like the Leopold Blake I know."

He forced a smile. "No, I mean: do you ever think people will stop coming at me? Stop trying to destroy the people I care about?"

"It's been getting worse, hasn't it?" She didn't phrase it as a question.

"Yes."

"This Chemworks business. Is it really as big a threat as Kate thinks it is?"

He paused. "Yes."

"What the hell were you mixed up in, Leopold?"

"I told you, I had no idea. The law was designed to shut me out. It couldn't be helped. Not with Harris working against me. But if someone's willing to pay that much money for a research company that hasn't turned a profit since it was founded…"

"Then there must be something valuable there," she said.

They both stood in silence for a moment. The wind picked up, whistling through the iron lattices. Most of the tourists had gone.

"Well, it sounds like a job for another day," said Mary. "We're in Paris, dammit. And I'm not going to let this ruin my vacation." She took Leopold's hand.

He felt the skin on his arms prickle. "Maybe we should go find the others."

"Or maybe you should just shut up a minute and appreciate the moment."

Leopold squeezed her hand. "Yes, ma'am."

They both turned and looked out over the horizon. The sun had shifted from pink to orange and the sky was nearly black. At street level, endless lines of red and white car lights snaked through the city in all directions. On the lawns below, couples gathered to pick out an empty spot of grass for the tower's nightly illuminations display.

Mary squeezed his hand back. "When we get back to New York, we'll get this all figured out. Until then, how about we enjoy ourselves a little?"

Leopold smiled. "I'll do my best."

"There's just one thing."

"What?"

"On no account am I eating snails. Or frog's legs. Or that thing with the raw beef and the egg. I just want to put that out there right now."

"I read about a place nearby that does a killer cheeseburger."

Mary smiled and drew in closer. "Sounds perfect."

"Then it's agreed." He felt the warmth from her body pressed up against his. "Cheeseburgers and beer. The perfect French experience."

"I think I've had all the French experience I can handle for now. Count me in."

"Sophie won't approve."

"She'll get over it."

Leopold didn't reply, instead pulling Mary in a little closer. The cold wind was making his face numb, but he barely noticed. He felt her body against his. She didn't pull away.

"Mary…"

She looked up into his eyes.

"About Kate. What did she say when you called her back?"

Mary let go of Leopold's hand. "Seriously? You want to talk about that now?" She pulled away.

"I just thought –"

"That's just the problem; you think too much." Turning on her heel, she walked away toward the elevators.

Leopold sighed, his breath condensing in front of his face. "Okay, okay, just wait a minute."

She stopped and glanced back.

He walked toward her. "You're right."

"About what?" She raised one eyebrow.

"That whatever's coming is coming and there's nothing we can do about it. That we should just live for the moment." He stopped as he drew close. "You know, just jump in feet first and let the universe figure out the details."

Mary folded her arms. "Maybe there's hope for you yet," she said. "Not much, mind you. But it's better than nothing."

"I'll take that as a compliment."

"Good. Because that's about as complimentary as I'm ever going to get." She shivered. "It's cold up here. Seeing as you've ruined the moment completely, what do you say we go find the others and get something to eat?"

Leopold rubbed his palms together to warm them up. "How about we just give it a few more minutes?" He took hold of her hands. "How's that?"

Mary moved in closer. "Better."

He let the moment fall into silence, holding on to each second as it passed by. The night didn't seem quite so cold, and, for the first time in his life, there was nowhere else he would rather be.

EPILOGUE: FIVE DAYS LATER

Luca Ginelli stepped into the decontamination chamber. He heard the airlock engage and saw the vents in the ceiling open, releasing concentrated plumes of vaporized hydrogen peroxide into the sealed room. Protected by the hazmat suit, the corrosive fumes posed no threat – except to the potential contagions that may have found their way onto the surface of his outfit.

The vents closed and the exhaust outlet slid open, sucking the poisonous air out of the chamber. A green light flashed to indicate the room was safe and Luca pulled off the protective suit, hanging it on one of the wall hooks. He opened one of the lockers and pulled out his lab clothes, quickly changing into them before heading for the exit. Sliding the bolt open, the young technician pulled on the handle and felt resistance. It wouldn't budge. He tried again, rattling the mechanism with mounting frustration. A faint hissing noise made Luca stop.

Did the airlock fail to engage properly? he thought, looking around the chamber. The green light was still flashing, signaling the environment was safe. He shrugged and tried the door again. No luck.

Peering through the glass, Luca strained to make out the room beyond. Thanks to the bright fluorescent bulbs inside the decon room, all he could see what his own reflection. He looked tired. After several weeks of pulling late shifts and sleeping at the lab he wasn't surprised, but the face of the man looking back at him was barely recognizable.

Luca almost jumped out of his skin when the face smiled at him.

"Jesus Christ!" his voice echoed against the cold steel of the chamber.

A light flicked on outside and the technician realized there was a man standing on the other side of the door, one he'd never seen before. He was tall and slim, with a hardened expression and a chiseled face. There were faint scars around his forehead and chin. The initial shock wearing off, Luca regained his composure and stared into the stranger's dark eyes. He immediately wished he hadn't.

"*Dottore* Ginelli," the man said. "I wanted to take the opportunity to speak with you before you retired for the evening."

Luca heard the man's voice through the intercom system. The stranger spoke with an accent, a mixture of dialects that the technician couldn't quite figure out. What was unmistakable, however, was the man's tone – somewhere between polite and menacing, the vocal equivalent of a switchblade wrapped in silk.

"Who are you?" asked Luca, forcing himself not to stammer. "This is a restricted area. You can't be down here." He felt his chest start to tighten, a common reaction whenever he was nervous.

"I beg to differ, *Dottore*." The man held up a security pass.

Luca wiped the back of his hand across his nose. "Who are you?" he repeated.

"Please excuse my manners. You might have been aware of the recent change in ownership?"

The technician nodded.

"Well, I'm here to make sure the company I bought is going to be worth the investment. You've been doing some very interesting work. I've been reading your case files. Impressive." He flashed a smile, although the expression was cold.

"Then you'll also know the experiments were a failure."

"Oh?"

"The nanoparticles we engineered targeted healthy cells as well as mutated ones. They destroyed everything they came into contact with. It was a complete failure."

"I wouldn't call that a failure, *Dottore*."

Luca rubbed his temples, feeling a migraine coming on. "In what world would you call it a success? Instead of developing a new way to target and destroy cancer cells, we created something even worse than the disease we were trying to cure. I recommended that the research be shut down and the results made public. We could learn a lot from the way this new virus works."

"That's not an option, I'm afraid." The man sighed. "You've done some wonderful work, as have your colleagues, but I'm afraid it's time for you to move on."

"What are you talking about?"

"Your work has been exemplary, and we appreciate the results you've given us. Unfortunately, some information has recently come to my attention that paints you in a rather negative light."

Luca felt the tightness in his chest get worse. "What information?"

"We monitor all incoming and outgoing cell phone signals here. I understand you've been having some conversations with the World Health Organization. That kind of behavior won't be tolerated."

"My rights are protected by international law," said Luca, stepping closer to the glass window. "Unlock this door. I'll be gone by the morning and you can discuss this with my union representative."

"Your union representative is otherwise engaged. And I'm afraid you won't be going anywhere." He rapped a knuckle on the glass. "Tell me, how are you feeling?"

Luca coughed into his hands, feeling something warm and wet against his palms.

"I thought as much," the man said. "Your work with viruses has been fascinating, but where they excel in terms of transmissibility and virulence, they can often take hours, or even days to reach full strength."

Luca looked down at his hands. They were covered in a brownish-red mucus. His migraine intensified as he tried to take a deep breath. He felt his heart begin to pump faster.

"For speedier results on a smaller scale, it made sense to look elsewhere." The man kept his dark eyes fixed on the technician as he spoke. "Some of your colleagues have been doing some wonderful things with synthetic nerve agents." He smiled again.

His head spinning, Luca dropped to his knees. "What the hell have you done?" he said, struggling to force enough air through his lungs to form the words.

"You can consider yourself the first human test subject for our latest breakthrough. It's based largely on the VX nerve agent, but we've made it a little bit nastier, as I'm sure you can tell." He paused. "We've not been able to come up with a name for it yet. Any ideas?"

Luca didn't reply, succumbing to a coughing fit. He could scarcely catch his breath.

"Never mind. I'm sure we'll think of something. The nerve agent we released through the vents is preventing all the muscles in your body from receiving signals from your brain. Following a period of intense muscle contraction," he let the words sink in, "your body will shut down entirely. I'm afraid it won't be pleasant."

The urge to cough faded and Luca felt his throat start to close up. "Wh-who the hell are you?" he said, as the tightness increased. It felt as though he were being strangled by invisible hands.

"I suppose that's a fair question." He stepped closer to the glass so that his breath left a fog.

Luca tried to speak but couldn't. His chest felt as though it were made of stone, and his futile attempts to breathe only intensified the pain in his skull. His heart started to pound more violently, struggling to deal with the shock of what was happening. The searing pain inside his lungs made him want to scream, but nothing came out. Then the pain stopped.

In the moments before his death, Luca Ginelli's life didn't flash before his eyes. He didn't ponder his regrets or wonder what might have been, he didn't even picture his family and friends. He only noticed the stranger at the window speaking the last words he would ever hear:

"My name is Robert. Robert Blake."

THE END

LEOPOLD BLAKE
WILL RETURN

Have you checked out the other books in the Leopold Blake series of thrillers?

For updates about new releases, as well as exclusive promotions, visit the author's website and sign up for the VIP mailing list at:

http://www.nickstephensonbooks.com